UNWIN HYMAN SHORT STORIES

ROUND

INCLUDING
FOLLOW ON
ACTIVITIES

EDITED BY ROY BLATCHFORD

Published by
Collins Educational, 77–85 Fulham Palace Road,
London W6 8JB
An imprint of HarperCollins*Publishers*

First published in 1985 by Bell & Hyman

Reprinted 1987, 1990, 1992

Selection and notes © Roy Blatchford, 1985

British Library Cataloguing in Publication Data

Unwin Hyman short stories
Round 2
I. Blatchford, Roy
428.6   PE1119

ISBN 0 00 322286 1

Printed in Great Britain by Billing & Sons Ltd, Worcester

Contents

Introduction

The eleven short stories in this collection have been chosen as suitable for pupils in the lower and middle years of secondary school. First of all, they should appeal as good plain story-telling and are perhaps best enjoyed when read aloud and shared with a group of pupils. But the stories also deal with a variety of ideas, subjects and situations about which pupils should be encouraged to reflect, and which can serve as starting points for their own story and play writing.

The stories are not grouped thematically but an idea encountered in one can readily be linked with another. There is no need to move chronologically through the collection, though 'The Toad' and 'The Aggie Match' have been placed at the end because they represent perhaps a more sophisticated type of story.

In looking for ways to approach the stories in the classroom, 'The Last Laugh', 'Lenny's Red-Letter Day' and 'The Choice Is Yours' could be taken together as lively and thought-provoking accounts of school-life. 'How The Elephant Became' and 'Sharlo's Strange Bargain' take the reader into the world of myth, legend and folklore, while 'The Toad' and 'The Hitch-hiker' (in characteristic Roald Dahl vein) have about them elements of the sinister and fantastic.

'Jeffie Lemmington and Me', 'Joe's Cat' and 'The Aggie Match' might be read alongside each other if pupils want to explore themes of loneliness, friendship, even prejudice. 'May Queen' is quite simply a splendidly warm and atmospheric tale of childhood pranks and could, in turn, be linked with the previously unpublished story 'The Last Laugh'.

In compiling this volume care has been taken to balance women and men writers and, equally important, bring to pupils stories which have both female and male protagonists. The Follow On section includes some simply-written notes so that teachers can help young readers discuss and appreciate the short story genre, together with a variety of supporting material to take readers into and beyond each of the eleven stories. Most of the stories have introductions by the authors, specially written for *Round Two*, which should prove of particular interest in discussion.

But the intention is *not* to perform a critical autopsy on what pupils have read. Rather, the stories are here to be read, shared and enjoyed – and, where it seems appropriate, used as springboards for extended language activities.

R. B.

May Queen

Gene Kemp

Farmer Woolley's field, the twelve acre, has two ponds in it. One is a perfectly ordinary pond at the side of the road that runs past the field, with nothing remarkable about it except a large hawthorn bush on its bank with pink blossom instead of white, and an iron rail that we turned somersaults on – all of us except Dawn Taylor. She couldn't manage to get over, not that she was fat, but she had no spring in her, no spring at all, being heavy, big-boned and solid. This sounds awful, but really she was a very pretty girl with long dark-brown hair, blue eyes, a straight nose and a perfect Cupid's bow mouth.

'I have a perfect Cupid's bow mouth, my mother says,' she would sometimes announce to us, as she stood looking in the cloakroom mirror at school. And since I have a great, big, gobby one, with the kind of teeth people call Tombstones, this did not greatly endear her to me. Nor did her being chosen as May Queen by our new Head-teacher, who was keen on bringing back he festivals to our village. I didn't think much of this May Queen stuff, it sounded dead boring to me, and what with specs and tombstones it didn't seem likely that I'd be chosen and I wasn't. But I didn't fancy being an attendant either, which is what I ended up as. Dawn is all right, really, with a nice nature, rather like a spaniel, and it's difficult to be horrible to her for long, though I did my best, being fed up at the thought of carrying her train and so on, for I did feel that being an attendant to anyone so stupid, however sweet-tempered, was a bit much. My partner in this train-bearing was a girl called Joan, bright and with-it, that one, but living outside the village in the new housing estate, so I did not play with her so often as Dawn.

1

Who, by now, had started to get really uppity, being an important figure at rehearsals, and what is worse, she had taken to reciting the items of her regalia, yes, she called it that, her crown, her sceptre, her orb, her velvet train, her long white gloves, her white satin dress, her seed-pearl necklace – what a load of boring rubbish, I said – but she took no notice as she continued with a long description of buying her white shoes and the man in the shop telling her mother that Dawn had the highest-arched foot he had ever seen. So have horses, I said, but she only looked at me as if I were some low, primeval form of life, and went on talking about her regalia. I shall go mad, I thought, as I rushed away and kicked a tree, which didn't hurt it at all, whereas I had to put a plaster on my blackened big toe.

I was to be dressed in yellow, a good colour on wasps, but hideous on me. My request to be allowed to keep my jeans on underneath the long frilled skirt was not considered, and Joan looked even worse in yellow than I did, being freckled with more freckles than spaces if you see what I mean. She was totally uninterested in the whole project as she was sailing to Australia soon after, and did nothing but talk about Australia, so, what with Australia and regalia, I found the pair of them jolly boring, and escaped from them and the never-ending rehearsals as often as possible.

The evening before the great day found me in my favourite field, Farmer Woolley's, the twelve acre, you remember, that's a really big field, with Jeff Hobbs. I've never been Jeff's girl-friend, in fact Dawn was really, but I liked him much better than Steve Coates, who is supposed to be mine, I don't know why, as I haven't been able to stand the sight of him since we were both about five. Anyway, Jeff's a bit thick but nice. Boys do not have to be bright as long as they are good company and dishy. Well, that evening, Jeff and I made our way to the *other* pond in Woolley's field. Quite different, this one, from the road-side pond with the pink blossom and the iron rail that Dawn can't somersault over. This pond had atmosphere. This pond had mystery.

It was in the far corner of the field, and on the other side of it was a curving path, that rose quite high above it, and this path was so covered by bushes and plants and moss and shaded by tall, arching trees that, unless you knew, you would never have guessed that it was there at all. On the other side of this path was a smaller pond that shelved into a corn-field. Beside the ponds was a grove of beeches set in a strange circle that looked as if it meant something though I've no idea what, and I called the whole place Wonderland, which wasn't clever or original, but no one else thought up anything better. It was always dark in that corner of the field, the water had a blackish-green tinge beneath the trees, whose twisted and bulgy roots stretched deep into the pond, with moss growing up their trunks. Here even the flowers were different – not buttercups, daisies and dandelions like the rest (which was growing for hay) but Jack-by-the-Hedge and Lords and Ladies (you should have heard what Jeff called those) and a poisonous plant called Deadly Night-shade we weren't supposed to touch. But, best of all, over the further pond, which was supposed to be bottomless since it never dried up in summer like the other ones, there lay a round pole, like a telegraph pole, reaching from one side to the other, from the hidden path to the bank in the field.

We were going along to see if there were any interesting new developments in the way of nests or tadpoles, and we made our way very quietly and secretly round the edge of the field, almost under the hedge, because Farmer Woolley did not care for anyone in his field when it was growing for hay, so we were Indians pathfinding a new trail, and this took a long time, twelve acres being a fair-sized field as I said before, and when we arrived we climbed a tree to see if there were any Palefaces lurking.

One well-known Paleface was. Wobbling and stately, Dawn was slowly making her way round the outside. Instant boredom woke inside me.

'I thought she was having her hair done and then going to bed early,' I sighed. However, as she approached we gave a wild Apache War Whoop and leapt off the branch together, just managing to miss her.

When she'd stopped screeching and got her breath back, we went on to the secret path, and sat on a mossy stump, looking at the pole lying so temptingly just above the green water. And, at that moment, two minds with but a single thought, Jeff and I decided that Dawn was going to walk across it. She hadn't said so, in fact she didn't know it as yet, but we knew. She had never yet dared to cross that pole. Tonight she would. Brave Dawn.

'I called for you,' she told me reproachfully.

'You told me you were having a shampoo and blow-dry.'

'I did. Don't you like it?'

'I liked it before. Straight.'

'I needed waves and curls to keep the crown in place.'

During this incredibly boring conversation Jeff got up and ran casually over the pole. There was no danger. He'd done it hundreds of times. The bottomless water gleamed green and cool.

'I'm wearing make-up tomorrow. Are you?'

'No.'

'Well, I suppose it won't make much difference in your case. You could leave off your glasses, though.'

I did not push her straight in. Instead I asked:

'How come you were let out?' Unlike Jeff and me, Dawn was an only, and the pride and joy of her mum and dad.

'I can only come for a moment. I felt all nervy, so my Mum said go and have a breath of fresh air, it will do you good, she said. I shall have to go back in a minute and check my regalia. The purple cloak, the white satin dress . . .' and she was off, reciting again.

Jeff crossed the log once more. I waited till he got to the other side, then I joined him, crossing over mid-way. We'd practised that one before, and it's fine as long as you don't look down. Seated on her mossy stump, Dawn had just reached the seed pearl necklace . . .

'What are you doing that for?' she burst out.

'For luck.'

'What luck?'

'This pond is enchanted. That's why it's called Wonder-

4

land. And a dragon lives down in a secret cave in the water below, and on May Eve, that's now, you have to cross over the pole or he won't like it.'

'What will he do?'

'He'll give you horrible bad luck.'

'What sort of bad luck?'

'Oh, like breaking your ankle getting out of bed, if you're going to be a Queen in a procession or something like that. Or falling flat on your face with everybody laughing at you except your mother who's crying.'

She was listening hard. At least, she'd stopped going through the regalia.

'I think I'd better go home now,' she said, standing up.

'Just walk over the pole then, and it will all be all right.'

'I don't want to.'

'It's nothing,' Jeff said. 'Easy as falling off a log.' I gave him a dirty look. Fine help he is. Dawn had got her mulish look.

'I don't believe in bad luck. My dad says it's all rubbish.'

And suddenly, I was worried stiff, for this seemed to be a dangerous thing to say in Wonderland on May Eve. Was I imagining the trees stirring and clouds passing over the sun, a sudden chill in the air?

'You'd better walk over the log now, Dawn, or you may really get bad luck. I can just imagine the dragon, full of anger, down there.'

I could too, by now, although I'd only just made him up.

Still she dithered.

'Come on, Dawnie,' Jeff sang out from the other side. 'I'll be here, to catch your hand.'

He grinned. He has a nice grin, and Dawn took a cautious step towards him, and began to cross, too slowly, too nervously. Half-way across she wobbled and looked down at the still, mysterious, dragon-haunted, bottomless water. It was too much. She wobbled furiously.

'I'm coming,' shouted Jeff.

'Don't look down!' I yelled.

She never did do what I told her. Jeff reached her too late,

5

as astonishingly slowly, like a great pigeon, she leaned from one side to the other and fell . . . phlomph . . .

The water wasn't bottomless, of course, and somehow she heaved over to the bank, where we hauled her in, and there she was, safe, but squelching, wearing what looked like mud boots from the knees down. We were all plastered with mud, and Dawn's hair had lost most of its curl. We stared at each other. I waited for Dawn to cry – she was bound to – I didn't blame her.

And she started to laugh. So did we. There on that bank, dripping with mud, we laughed and laughed and laughed.

'I'm sorry . . .' I spluttered, 'about . . . hahahaha . . . your . . . hair . . . hahaha.'

'I don't care.' She was half-way between laughing and crying. 'I was sick of May Queening, anyway, and everybody hating the sight of me and being horrible. Bother the regalia.'

Jeff recovered first, struggling to his feet.

'Home,' he said. He never talked much.

So we set off round the never-ending outside of the twelve-acre field, dragging a bit, especially Dawn on her mud feet. When we neared the last stile I said let's cut across the corner, and we were almost there, when a figure appeared, gaunt, menacing, stick in hand.

'Farmer Woolley! Run for it! Quick!'

We ran. Like murder, me in front. I flung myself over the stile just as Jeff and Dawn came up behind, Jeff tugging her along. Somehow, on the stile they collided, banged heads, and fell, a mixed-up heap. Jeff rolled nearly into the grass, but Dawn, as I told you, has no spring, no spring at all. Down she fell, like a cartload of bricks, splat . . .

The following day, the May Queen walked proudly but slowly and stiffly in front of her attendants. That was because her right knee and left ankle were heavily bandaged. Make-up hid the bruise on her forehead, though not the plaster on her nose. Her hair was straight and a bit tatty, but her cheeks were pink and she smiled beautifully at the photographers and admiring friends and relations from her perfect Cupid's bow mouth (undamaged). A great cheer went up for her.

Behind her followed a tall girl with freckles, and a small wicked-looking one with specs and big teeth. Mrs. Taylor has an enormous coloured photo of it all in the place of honour in their front room. We've only got a little one at home, but I don't mind.

The Last Laugh

Gervase Phinn

Miss Sculthorpe gave one of her famous smiles. It stretched from ear to ear like the grinning green frog in the tank on the nature table. When she stopped smiling we expected to see lipstick on her ears. Next to her was a pale, blond-haired boy with blue eyes.

'Will you all look this way, please?' said Miss Sculthorpe. 'And that includes you, Jason Johnson. Thank you. Now this morning we have a new addition to our class.'

She turned in the direction of the new boy and her smile seemed to stretch even wider.

'This is Hans. He doesn't speak very much English because he's from another country, so you will all have to speak slowly for him to understand you. Now Hans is only with us for two weeks but during that time I'm sure you will all make him feel at home.'

'Where's he from, Miss?' asked Valerie Clamp, her hand waving like a daffodil in the wind.

'I'm just about to tell you, Valerie dear, if you'll let me finish.'

The new boy stared around the room with a blank expression on his face. If I'd have been up there in front of all the class with all those eyes on me I'd have been bright red. But he just stood there as calm as anything. I don't suppose he understood a word Miss Sculthorpe was saying.

'Can anyone guess which country Hans comes from? His name should give you a clue.'

'Is he from Ireland, Miss?' asked Martin Mullane. 'My cousin's from Ireland and she's got a funny name. My dad says my uncle Michael wants his head examining calling her that.'

'Hans is not a funny name, Martin. In fact it's quite a common name in his country.'

'Miss, my cousin's name's Attracta,' Martin Mullane went on.

'Blimey!' Micky Lincoln piped in. 'Fancy calling somebody a tractor! What's her brother called – a combine harvester?'

'No!' spluttered Martin. 'Not a tractor like the one you drive round a farm. It's all one word – Attracta. Twit!'

'That will do, Martin. Now Hans is not from Ireland. People in Ireland speak English.'

'Miss,' said Martin, 'that's not what my dad says. He says he can't understand a word they say when we visit my Auntie Monica in Belfast.'

'Thank you very much, Martin. I think we've heard quite enough about your Irish relations. Now Hans is from Germany.'

Miss Sculthorpe turned to the new boy and did an imitation of the frog again.

'Now there's an empty place next to John Mullarkey, so you can sit there.' She pointed to the seat next to mine.

'And you'll look after Hans for today, won't you, John?'

'Yes, miss,' I replied.

'And remember he doesn't speak much English so you will have to point to things and speak slowly.'

Then the German boy spoke.

'I understand very much what you are saying. I learn to speak English in my school in Germany.'

'Well,' said Miss Sculthorpe, 'that will make things a lot easier, Hans.'

'In my school in Germany I learn English with Herr Dahlinger. I learn it for two years.'

'And you speak it very well too,' said Miss Sculthorpe. 'Now you sit next to John and he'll tell you all about the school.'

'What's your second name?' I asked.

'Please?'

'Your other name. Hans what?'

'Hans Von Kobberger.'

'Crikey! That's a mouthful.'

'What is this mouthful?'

'You know – a lot to say. Bit like Mullarkey really.'

'Ja.'

'Whereabouts in Germany are you from?'

'Baden-Baden.'

'Never heard of it.'

'It is much bigger than your town.'

'Yes, I suppose it's a lot different over here.'

'It does not rain with all the vinds and it is not cold.'

'Oh, it's all right in summer.'

'I am also not liking the *Gestank*.'

'The what?'

He made a sniffing noise.

'Oh, that, the smell you mean. Oh, you get used to that. It's from the knacker's yard.'

'*Bitte?*'

'The knacker's yard. They get loads of old bones and boil 'em up to make glue. If the wind's in the wrong direction there's a right pong. Course, it could be the sewage works on Midden Road or Demoulder's Maggot Farm on Common Lane.'

By this time Miss Sculthorpe had got all her materials together and was ready to start the first lesson which was my favourite – English.

'Will you all look this way, please?'

Most of us stopped talking.

'And that includes you, Jason Johnson.'

Silence.

'This morning I want you all to think about the sea. I know the summer holidays are a long way off but on a dull and rainy day like this it's rather nice to think about the sun and sand and sea.'

'Miss!'

'Yes, what is it, Barry?'

'Miss, my dad nearly got drowned last year at Morecambe. He was swept out to sea on this twenty-foot wave . . .'

10

We all burst out laughing.

'Miss, it's true, he was on a Lilo and he fell asleep.'

'Miss,' shouted Valerie Clamp. 'Miss, my sister was bitten by a jellyfish last year when she was in Spain.'

'Well, I don't think jellyfish actually bite, Valerie,' replied Miss Sculthorpe. 'They sting but I really don't think they . . .'

'Miss, they do,' said Valerie. 'There was a big red blotch on her leg where it bit her.'

The class again burst into laughter.

'Miss, we've been to Spain,' said Micky Lincoln. 'And when we were coming through customs, they stopped my grandma and made her go in this room and take all her clothes off.'

Miss Sculthorpe turned to Hans who was staring out of the window.

'Do you live near the sea, Hans?'

'No.'

'Do you go on holidays to the seaside?'

'Ja, but in Germany it is hot and there are not the vinds mit der pong.'

'With the what?'

'He means the smell, Miss. Probably from the maggot farm on Common Lane.'

'Thank you, John. I don't know how we managed to get on to maggot farms. I started talking about the sea. Anyway, I've brought in a collection of sea shells this morning and in a minute I'm going to put some on each desk. Now I want you to look very closely at the shells, notice what colours there are and the shape and feel, and then we are going to write a poem or a description – a sort of picture in words. Yes, what is it now, Martin?'

'Miss, last year when we were on holiday at my Auntie Monica's in Belfast, we went to this place called Bangor and my cousin Attracta stood on a shell and her foot swelled up like a balloon and went all purple and yellow and she had to go into hospital where this doctor got this kind of knife thing and cut right into her . . .'

11

'Thank you, Martin, I've already told you that we've heard quite enough of your Irish relations for one day. Now I want you all to write a colourful and interesting poem or short description about your shell. For example, this one is pink and smooth and rounded. This one is flat and bumpy with tiny holes in it, and this one on Barry's desk is sharp and spikey and blue. So I want you all to look very closely at your shell and use your imaginations.'

Miss Sculthorpe then went round the classroom giving out shells of all sizes and shapes and colours. Soon we had settled down to work and all you could hear was the scratching of pens. After ten minutes I had written about half a page and was very pleased with my effort:

> I can see a white shell, clean and polished,
> It curls and twists and shines like a pearl.
> There are tiny grains of sand clinging to it
> And it smells of the sea.

I looked at Hans' paper. It hadn't a thing written on it. He was staring out of the window and looked as bored as my mum when the football's on the telly. I looked over to where Miss Sculthorpe was whispering loudly in Martin Mullane's ear.

'You just did not listen, did you, Martin? I asked for a poem or a short description about a shell, not a story about a killer clam which devours deep sea divers and spits out their bones. Now start again and do as you were told.'

'Yes, Miss.'

Then Miss Sculthorpe headed in my direction. She peered over my shoulder.

'Oh yes, I like this, John. You describe your shell very well.' Then she caught sight of Hans who was still looking out of the window.

'Didn't you understand what you had to do, Hans?' she asked.

'Ja, but I do not do it!'

'I beg your pardon?' The smile on Miss Sculthorpe's face suddenly disappeared.

12

'This is not the proper English. This is, how do you say, my waste of time.'

Miss Sculthorpe's face was now sort of screwed up as if she was sucking a lemon. Her neck was all red and blotchy. The last time she had looked like that was when Barry Bannister had let the rat out of its cage and it had ended up in her shopping bag.

'Not the proper English? Tell me, Hans, what is the proper English?' She said the last three words really slowly. Everyone was now looking at Hans.

'In Germany with Herr Dahlinger, we learn the proper English. Before I am coming to England I learn about the proberbs.'

'Really? The proberbs,' repeated Miss Sculthorpe.

'My English teacher, Herr Dahlinger, he tests the proberbs. A bird in the hands is worth two in the bushes; every cloud has the silver lining; people what are in the glass houses should not be throwing the stones; it is like a pig in a china poke.'

'Well, for your information, Hans, English people rarely use *proverbs* any more.'

'Herr Dahlinger says all English people use proberbs.'

'Well, I'm afraid Herr Dahlinger is wrong. Very few people use proverbs these days.'

'Herr Dahlinger also he teaches me about the verbs and the nouns and the sentences. This is the proper English.'

Miss Sculthorpe breathed out. We could see she was really mad.

'Well, Hans dear,' she said quietly, 'it won't be long now before you are back in the classroom of the excellent Herr Dahlinger learning the "proper" English, but until then you are in my classroom and you must follow the very famous proverb which I am sure you are only too familiar with: When in Rome you do as the Romans do. So get on with your description of your shell.'

Over the next two weeks Hans didn't find much to his liking. The Headmaster was 'a *Dummkopf*', the school dinners were 'only for the pigs', the games teacher could not

13

'referee a game of tiddlivinks'. He refused to let the nit nurse look at his hair – 'German people do not have the creatures on the head' – or the school dentist examine his teeth. When the school photographer asked him to 'smile please' he replied: 'What is there to be smiling at?' He was a real pain in the neck. And he went on and on about Miss Sculthorpe not teaching the proper English.

It was a bright and sunny day when Mr Morgan, the Headmaster, came into our classroom.

'Now will you all look this way a moment. And that includes you, Jason Johnson. Now some of you may know that next Monday, the 24th of October, is United Nations Day and I thought it would be a good idea – he was full of good ideas was Mr Morgan – 'to have an assembly with an international flavour at which we could have some prayers in different languages.'

Then he looked to where Hans was sitting.

'Perhaps, Hans, you might like to read a prayer in German?' We all expected him to shake his head but to our surprise he agreed.

'Ja, I will read. I will read something special.'

'Splendid, splendid,' said Mr Morgan rubbing his hands.

On the Monday morning we all filed into the hall for the assembly. It had been decorated by Mr Wilson and his third-year class with flags of all nations and pictures of people in different costumes. Large coloured posters were pinned all round the stage which was full of children. In the centre stood Hans as calm as ever.

First to read was Rahila Ahmed with an Islamic prayer, then Jamuna Mahjaran read a poem in Nepalese. Audrey Jaworski sang a Ukranian song and Li Kong said something in Chinese.

Then it was Hans' turn.

In a loud voice he went on and on in German. I think it was the first time I'd seen him smile. At first there was a little twist at the corners of his mouth but then it spread into a wide grin. At last we all mumbled Amen. Mr Morgan stood up and thanked all the readers. Then he went on about loving your neighbour and that we were all sisters and brothers whatever our colour or religion or country.

'It was just like listening to my Auntie Monica,' said Martin Mullane on the way out of the hall. 'I didn't understand a word.'

'Here,' I said to Hans when we got back to the classroom. 'That prayer of yours went on a bit. I thought you were never going to stop.'

'What prayer?' he said.

'The one you read in assembly. You must spend half of your time in church back in Germany with prayers like that.'

'It was not a prayer,' he said.

'Not a prayer?'

'No, I do not know any prayers.'

'What were you saying then?' I asked.

Hans thought for a moment and then a smile spread across his face.

'I said the Headmaster is a fool. I said the school dinners are like the food for pigs. I said England is cold and stinks and I said the English teacher does not teach the proper English.'

'Crikey! You said all that?'

'Ja.'

The thought of all of us saying Amen to that little lot brought a smile to my face. We must have looked a comical pair when Miss Sculthorpe walked in.

'My, my,' she said, 'you two look happy today.' Then she looked at Hans.

'Remember the old English proverb, won't you Hans: He who laughs last laughs the longest.'

'Oh ja,' said Hans in such an innocent voice.

'And what are you laughing at, John Mullarkey?' asked Miss Sculthorpe.

Jeffie Lemmington And Me

Merle Hodge

I was seven and I had thought that snow was like cotton
wool, so I had always wondered how the children in books
made snowmen stand up without the breeze blowing them
away.

When my mother woke me up one morning, she said,
'There's snow, darling, come and see!'

We stood at the window looking down. The tops of the
parked cars were covered with thick white hair, as though
they had grown old in the night. The pavement was covered
with it, too, and the roof – the long row of joined-together
roofs – of the opposite side of the street, everything. It was
very mysterious. A giant had come and quietly laid his fluffy
white towel down over the whole street and vanished again.

My mother was holding me. 'Pretty, eh?' she said. I did
not answer. Instead I squirmed with shyness. I was shy of my
mother. I did not know my mother, I did not know my
father, and – I did not trust the little boy they had with them
who did not talk like me and didn't seem to feel cold, who
they said was my little brother.

I had looked forward to seeing my little brother. When I
was going to take the plane, Granny had given me a paperbag
full of sweets to bring for him. And he had sniffed and
nibbled at them, screwing up his face, and handed them
back to my mother.

In the night when I was falling asleep, or when I woke up

16

in the middle of the night, then this place seemed to be a dream that I was having. It was always close and dark here, as in a dream, and there was no midday; the whole day was the same colour. And you could never just scamper out through the front door if you felt like it, you had first to pile on all those clothes that made you feel heavier than when you had got soaked in the rain.

But when I was up and about, then it was Granny and Uncle Nello who seemed to be tucked away in a dream somewhere, or in some bright yellow storybook.

Granny was both sad and happy when they'd written and said that I could go to them now. Happy for me because at last I was going Up There. They were rather put out when I announced that I wasn't going anywhere. I hadn't the slightest interest in my mother and father – only when I got parcels from them with sweets and toys; but when I had gobbled up the sweets and broken the toys or exchanged them for things my friends had, then I forgot about my mother and father until the next parcel came.

But I didn't mind going Up There to have a look at this little brother who seemed to have crept into the world behind my back, for Granny and Uncle Nello said that I had never seen him. (They also said that I *had* seen my mother and father and that they had seen me, but I knew they were only fooling me.)

And now I had come to this uncomfortable place, and I had seen my little brother, and now I was ready to go back to Granny and Uncle Nello.

We put on all our clothes, my mother and I, and set out for school. But . . . snow was crunchy to walk on, like biscuit crumbs, not a bit like cotton wool! My mother was picking her way carefully along, and I soon discovered why. For we had made only a few steps when my shoes played a trick on me and I sat down in the snow. It was hard, and I stayed sitting and bellowed at the top of my voice. This was enough. I wanted to go home to Granny and Uncle Nello. Enough of this foolish place.

17

Every day my mother took me to school and came and fetched me in the afternoon. Even when I knew the way myself. I wanted to walk with Jeffie Lemmington. We lived on the same street. And besides, hardly anyone else's mother brought them to school and came to fetch them like babies. So on afternoons when I came through the school gates and out of the corner of my eye had checked to see that my mother was standing there, I then ignored her, and walked a little way behind her all the way home.

But after a while she stopped coming and then Jeffie Lemmington and I made our joyful way together to and from school. We walked along the tops of little garden walls, our arms cutting through the air like windmills; we played hide-and-seek in and out of the crowd along the street that was always full of people; when we had to cross the road, we stood on the pavement and held hands, and he looked to the left and I looked to the right, and then we raced over; we fished a tin can out of a dustbin and kicked it all the way home, enjoying the delightful noise it made on the concrete. And we played together at school, too, Jeffie Lemmington and me. When Jeffie Lemmington and I were playing together, then I almost forgot that I didn't like this place and wanted to go back to Granny and Uncle Nello.

One morning, Jeffie Lemmington did not meet me at our gate and I set out alone. Then I saw him a little way ahead of me and called happily to him as I charged down the street. But when I caught up with him, he looked at me miserably. 'My mum says I'm not to play with you,' he said, kicking a stone.

'Why?' I asked in astonishment.

'Because she says you prob'ly smell and you'll give me lice.'

'What is lice?'

His face brightened for a moment. 'Don' you know what lice is?' he said, sticking his chest out. 'Haw, I've 'ad lice heaps of times!'

Lice I pictured as some tempting dessert that wasn't really too good for you. His face fell again and we walked along thinking, trying to puzzle the whole thing out.

At recreation time we did not play, we stood near to each other on the playground with our hands in our pockets, each sadly kicking at a blade of grass or spinning slowly on one heel. Then suddenly Jeffie Lemmington stood stock still. 'I know what!' he said, running towards me. 'I'll take you to my mum so she can smell you, and when she smells you don't smell of anything, then we can play!' We hugged each other and danced round and round.

We could not wait for that schoolday to end. In the classroom we looked at each other every now and then and smiled. When school was over we burst out of the gates, almost dragging each other along by the hand as we pelted down the road.

Jeffie Lemmington was ringing the doorbell, still gripping my hand. A lady opened the door, smiling. But suddenly her mouth gasped like a fish's and her eyes grew wide, then her eyes got small and her mouth clamped together hard and angry, and I was terrified. And the next thing I knew Jeffie Lemmington's hand was pulled from mine and he was disappearing head first through the door by no will of his own, and BRAM I was standing in front of a dirty cream door in a cold passage in a strange house.

I dashed down the stairs as fast as my legs could carry me and ran all the way home, crying.

My mother said, with a strange look on her face, well that was that, I couldn't play with *him* any longer; maybe the best thing to do would be to find a little boy just like me to play with; there were some little boys like me at the school, weren't there? But Jeffie Lemmington *was* just like me! He was seven and he was going to be a footballer and he hated milk. But my mother clamped her mouth together and wouldn't say a word more.

I threw a tantrum. If I couldn't play with my friend Jeffie Lemmington, then I wasn't staying in this place any longer; I was going home. My little brother stood with his thumb in his mouth and stared, impressed, as I bravely kicked and writhed and roared. I made a face at him and he stepped back.

The next day, Jeffie Lemmington and I walked to school on opposite sides of the street. Every now and then we peeped sideways at each other; every time we came to a corner, each took a quick look to see that the other was crossing safely.

At recreation time we were standing near to each other again, kicking at pebbles, when I had an idea this time: 'Let's run away!'

What I had in mind was running away to Granny and Uncle Nello. Jeffie Lemmington said that we would run away to a farm and be farm-hands, shearing sheep and slaughtering cows, until we were older, then we'd become footballers, because they didn't take little boys of seven to be footballers. The idea wasn't a bad one, and at any rate I would go along with it until I could get back to Granny and Uncle Nello.

We would get on the train, and when we had been on the train long enough then we'd be in the country, where farms were, said Jeffie Lemmington. He knew, he'd been to the country once, to a farm.

We did not shoot out of the school gates as we had done the day before. But we held hands even more tightly than the day before. Looking neither right nor left, nor, above all, at each other, we set off down the road. At the corner where we usually crossed over, we firmly turned right instead, and after we had gone a few steps, we could look at each other and smile happily, and then break into a run.

Down in the Underground the escalators were a temptation, we *had* to ride on them for a bit. We rode up and down and backwards on the escalators until suddenly a million people were hurrying down the passage, clattering with their feet, and they filled up the escalator and there were still more coming; so we decided to continue on our way to the country.

And there wasn't much else we could do, for now we were being sucked along in a kind of wave, like the time when the sea grabbed me and was dragging me away when I was little,

but Uncle Nello had been there to pull me out; and Jeffie
Lemmington was terrified, too, for he held on to me as we
were carried forward.

But all of a sudden the crowd came loose and we were free.
We were on the train platform. We wanted to go home.

'Fun, ain't it?' squeaked Jeffie Lemmington.

'Yes, fun, ain't it?' I squeaked in agreement. A fearful
thundering – the train never thundered so when we were
down in the Underground with our mothers – and the giant
centipede rushed in.

We were pushed into it and we clutched each other again.
When the doors slid shut and locked us away, Jeffie Lemmington and I were standing pressed tightly together
stomach to stomach, so that we had to take turns drawing
breath.

We travelled like this for a long time, shaken to and fro,
not saying a word, until the train began to empty itself. 'I
think the next stop's the country,' came Jeffie Lemmington's
frightened voice.

We followed some people off the train and up the stairs,
walking quietly behind them so they wouldn't notice. We
were oozing through a small space in a barrier, and just as we
escaped to the other side a voice called out sharply:

'Tickets! You two! Come back here!'

'Run!' said Jeffie Lemmington; and we ran.

But at the door Jeffie Lemmington stood stock still and
looked as if he was going to cry. He was staring about. 'But
this isn't the country!' he said.

We had no idea how long we had been walking in the streets.
But it was dark now, and we were cold. There was food in
lighted windows. We had not spoken for a long time. We
were too frightened. We were more frightened than we were
hungry, or tired, or cold. Our mothers would never find us,
and what was going to become of us? I thought of my mother
and father and little brother sitting eating, indoors, in the
warm. How dare they! – when I was not there. Sometimes
people looked at us curiously.

21

Suddenly Jeffie Lemmington sat down, in the middle of the pavement, and bawled. Right away I dropped down beside him and did the same. We sat on the pavement side by side and bellowed at the tops of our voices. People passing stopped and stood around us, looking as if they were not sure what they should do; and then a lady bent down and asked us where we lived.

We don't really remember the ride in the police car, because by then we were fast asleep, but all the other boys think we do. We've told them how they let us blow the siren and make the light on top flash as we tore through the streets, and other cars had to move aside as we raced along . . . All we really remember is the lady taking us to her house and giving us dinner; and she tried to give us milk, and we fell asleep.

And then us in the newspaper. ' 'Ow do we know it's you?' said George Tiller, but he was only jealous. Of course he is right, maybe; if you didn't know, you'd think it was just some policemen and my mother and Jeffie Lemmington's mum holding two bundles with legs and looking right silly, laughing like twits.

And my mother has told *every*body, a million times (if you knew my mother, you'd expect her to tell one story a million times), how funny it was, when the policemen came in with the two bundles in blankets how they each rushed and grabbed one, and how the two bundles were exactly the same size and only our shoes and socks were showing, black shoes and grey socks with a green stripe – and if you knew my mother, you'd expect her to get the wrong bundle, and so did Jeffie Lemmington's mum. So that's why they're all laughing in the picture like twits. I wish they'd turned us around so everybody could see it *was* us, Jeffie Lemmington and me.

How The Elephant Became

Ted Hughes

The unhappiest of all the creatures was Bombo. Bombo didn't know what to become. At one time he thought he might make a fairly good horse. At another time he thought that perhaps he was meant to be a kind of bull. But it was no good. Not only the horses, but all the other creatures too, gathered to laugh at him when he tried to be a horse. And when he tried to be a bull, the bulls just walked away shaking their heads.

'Be yourself,' they all said.

Bombo sighed. That's all he ever heard: 'Be yourself. Be yourself.' What was himself? That's what he wanted to know.

So most of the time he just stood, with sad eyes, letting the wind blow his ears this way and that, while the other creatures raced around him and above him, perfecting themselves.

'I'm just stupid,' he said to himself. 'Just stupid and slow and I shall never become anything.'

That was his main trouble, he felt sure. He was much too slow and clumsy – and so big! None of the other creatures were anywhere near so big. He searched hard to find another creature as big as he was, but there was not one. This made him feel all the more silly and in the way.

But this was not all. He had great ears that flapped and hung, and a long, long nose. His nose was useful. He could pick things up with it. But none of the other creatures had a

23

nose anything like it. They all had small neat noses, and they laughed at his. In fact, with that, and his ears, and his long white sticking-out tusks, he was a sight.

As he stood, there was a sudden thunder of hooves. Bombo looked up in alarm.

'Aside, aside, aside!' roared a huge voice. 'We're going down to drink.'

Bombo managed to force his way backwards into a painful clump of thorn-bushes, just in time to let Buffalo charge past with all his family. Their long black bodies shone, their curved horns tossed, their tails screwed and curled, as they pounded down towards the water in a cloud of dust. The earth shook under them.

'There's no doubt,' said Bombo, 'who they are. If only I could be as sure of what I am as Buffalo is of what he is.'

Then he pulled himself together.

'To be myself,' he said aloud, 'I shall have to do something that no other creature does. Lion roars and pounces, and Buffalo charges up and down bellowing. Each of these creatures does something that no other creature does. So. What shall I do?'

He thought hard for a minute.

Then he lay down, rolled over on to his back, and waved his four great legs in the air. After that he stood on his head and lifted his hind legs straight up as if he were going to sunburn the soles of his feet. From this position, he lowered himself back on to his four feet, stood up and looked round. The others should soon get to know me by that, he thought.

Nobody was in sight, so he waited until a pack of wolves appeared on the horizon. Then he began again. On to his back, his legs in the air, then on to his head, and his hind legs straight up.

'Phew!' he grunted, as he lowered himself. 'I shall need some practice before I can keep this up for long.'

When he stood up and looked round him this second time, he got a shock. All the animals were round him in a ring, rolling on their sides with laughter.

24

'Do it again! Oh, do it again!' they were crying, as they rolled and laughed. 'Do it again. Oh, I shall die with laughter. Oh, my sides, my sides!'

Bombo stared at them in horror.

After a few minutes the laughter died down.

'Come on!' roared Lion. 'Do it again and make us laugh. You look so silly when you do it.'

But Bombo just stood. This was much worse than imitating some other animal. He had never made them laugh so much before.

He sat down and pretended to be inspecting one of his feet, as if he were alone. And, one by one, now that there was nothing to laugh at, the other animals walked away, still chuckling over what they had seen.

'Next show same time tomorrow!' shouted Fox, and they all burst out laughing again.

Bombo sat, playing with his foot, letting the tears trickle down his long nose.

Well, he'd had enough. He'd tried to be himself, and all the animals had laughed at him.

That night he waded out to a small island in the middle of the great river that ran through the forest. And there, from then on, Bombo lived alone, seen by nobody but the little birds and a few beetles.

One night, many years later, Parrot suddenly screamed and flew up into the air above the trees. All his feathers were singed. The forest was on fire.

Within a few minutes, the animals were running for their lives. Jaguar, Wolf, Stag, Cow, Bear, Sheep, Cockerel, Mouse, Giraffe – all were running side by side and jumping over each other to get away from the flames. Behind them, the fire came through the treetops like a terrific red wind.

'Oh dear! Oh dear! Our houses, our children!' cried the animals.

Lion and Buffalo were running along with the rest.

'The fire will go as far as the forest goes, and the forest goes on for ever,' they cried, and ran with sparks falling into their hair. On and on they ran, hour after hour, and all they could hear was the thunder of the fire at their tails.

On into the middle of the next day, and still they were running.

At last they came to the wide, deep, swift river. They could go no farther. Behind them the fire boomed as it leapt from tree to tree. Smoke lay so thickly over the forest and the river that the sun could not be seen. The animals floundered in the shallows at the river's edge, trampling the banks to mud, treading on each other, coughing and sneezing in the white ashes that were falling thicker than thick snow out of the cloud of smoke. Fox sat on Sheep and Sheep sat on Rhinoceros.

They all set up a terrible roaring, wailing, crying, howling, moaning sound. It seemed like the end of the animals. The fire came nearer, bending over them like a thundering roof, while the black river swirled and rumbled beside them.

Out on his island stood Bombo, admiring the fire which made a fine sight through the smoke with its high spikes of red flame. He knew he was quite safe on his island. The fire couldn't cross that great stretch of water very easily.

At first he didn't see the animals crowding low by the edge of the water. The smoke and ash were too thick in the air. But soon he heard them. He recognized Lion's voice shouting:

'Keep ducking yourselves in the water. Keep your fur wet and the sparks will not burn you.'

And the voice of Sheep crying:

'If we duck ourselves we're swept away by the river.'

And the other creatures – Gnu, Ferret, Cobra, Partridge, crying:

'We must drown or burn. Good-bye, brothers and sisters!'

It certainly did seem like the end of the animals.

Without a pause, Bombo pushed his way into the water. The river was deep, the current heavy and fierce, but Bombo's legs were both long and strong. Burnt trees, that had fallen into the river higher up and were drifting down, banged against him, but he hardly felt them.

26

In a few minutes he was coming up into shallow water towards the animals. He was almost too late. The flames were forcing them, step by step, into the river, where the current was snatching them away.

Lion was sitting on Buffalo, Wolf was sitting on Lion, Wildcat on Wolf, Badger on Wildcat, Cockerel on Badger, Rat on Cockerel, Weasel on Rat, Lizard on Weasel, Tree-Creeper on Lizard, Harvest Mouse on Tree-Creeper, Beetle on Harvest Mouse, Wasp on Beetle, and on top of Wasp, Ant, gazing at the raging flames through his spectacles and covering his ears from their roar.

When the animals saw Bombo looming through the smoke, a great shout went up:

'It's Bombo! It's Bombo!'

All the animals took up the cry:

'Bombo! Bombo!'

Bombo kept coming closer. As he came, he sucked up water in his long silly nose and squirted it over his back, to protect himself from the heat and the sparks. Then, with the same long, silly nose he reached out and began to pick up the animals, one by one, and seat them on his back.

'Take us!' cried Mole.

'Take us!' cried Monkey.

He loaded his back with the creatures that had hooves and big feet; then he told the little clinging things to cling on to the great folds of his ears. Soon he had every single creature aboard. Then he turned and began to wade back across the river, carrying all the animals of the forest towards safety.

Once they were safe on the island they danced for joy. Then they sat down to watch the fire. Suddenly Mouse gave a shout:

'Look! The wind is bringing sparks across the river. The sparks are blowing into the island trees. We shall burn here too.'

As he spoke, one of the trees on the edge of the island crackled into flames. The animals set up a great cry and began to run in all directions.

'Help! Help! Help! We shall burn here too!'

But Bombo was ready. He put those long silly tusks of his, that he had once been so ashamed of, under the roots of the burning tree and heaved it into the river. He threw every tree into the river till the island was bare. The sparks now fell on to the bare torn ground, where the animals trod them out easily. Bombo had saved them again.

Next morning the fire had died out at the river's edge. The animals on the island looked across at the smoking, blackened plain where the forest had been. Then they looked round for Bombo.

He was nowhere to be seen.

'Bombo!' they shouted. 'Bombo!' And listened to the echo.

But he had gone.

He is still very hard to find. Though he is huge and strong, he is very quiet.

But what did become of him in the end? Where is he now?

Ask any of the animals, and they will tell you:

'Though he is shy, he is the strongest, the cleverest, and the kindest of all the animals. He can carry anything and he can push anything down. He can pick you up in his nose and wave you in the air. We would make him our king if we could get him to wear a crown.'

Sharlo's Strange Bargain

Ralph Prince

In Glentis Village, when people notice that you love your belly, they often say: 'You belly goin' bring you to de same en' like Sharlo.' And then they will tell you the story of Sharlo and his strange bargain. It's an old, old story, and they say it's true. This is how it goes:

There once lived a man in Glentis Village named Sharlo. Some called him 'Long-belly Sharlo', because he loved food too much. Others called him 'Sharlo the Fifer', because he was the best fife player in the village. The fife was made from bamboo in Sharlo's own secret way, and it was the sweetest fife the villagers had ever heard. They believed that the music he played on it was the sweetest in all the world.

One afternoon Sharlo was returning home after working in his lands in the mountain. He was on the lower slopes, but still a long way from home, when a heavy shower of rain began to fall. He sheltered under a tree, but he got slightly wet all the time. The rain poured in torrents all afternoon and evening, enveloping the mountain in a thick, white sheet.

When darkness gathered, Sharlo felt cold and miserable. So he took out his fife and played it. He played all the old songs he could remember – songs of the old folk when they lived in the mountain, songs of the fishermen in Glentis Village, sad songs and merry songs. All these and more he played and played, sweeter than he had ever played before.

Then suddenly he stopped playing. Right before him

29

appeared a tall, red man. Sharlo was astonished, for he had not seen where the man had come from. 'Go ahead playing,' said the man. 'You played so sweet that I came up from down yonder to hear you.'

Sharlo asked him who he was, and the man said that everybody knew him. Sharlo then looked at him closely to see if he really knew him. The man seemed neither young nor old, but ageless. His skin was red and looked like the shell of a boiled lobster. His hair was white and flowing. His eyes were red, and they glowed as if fires burned within them. 'Never see you before,' said Sharlo, after looking at him searchingly and long.

'You will soon remember who I am,' declared the man, 'and you will get to know me more, Sharlo.'

'How you know me name?' asked Sharlo, in surprise.

'Aha!' laughed the man. 'I know everybody, Sharlo – everybody in this world!'

Meanwhile Sharlo was still getting wet, so he edged up closer to the trunk of the tree. But the rain ran off the man's body like water sliding off a duck's back.

'Would you like to come down to my place for shelter?' asked the man.

Sharlo wondered where that place was. But he was wet, and above all, hungry, so he agreed to go, hoping to get some food there. The man led the way and Sharlo followed. As fast as the man walked, a hole opened in the mountain before him, going downwards all the time.

At last he stopped. Sharlo found himself in a large, oven-like room with fires burning along the walls. It was so hot that his clothes soon became dry and he had to take off his shirt; but the man was not even sweating.

He offered Sharlo a chair before a table, and then sat facing Sharlo. The man said nothing, but watched him intently. Sharlo yawned several times, expecting the man to offer him something to eat. But the man just watched him intently and said nothing. At last Sharlo could bear it no longer. 'You got any food?' he asked.

'Plenty,' the man replied. 'I was waiting for you to ask for some.' He then put a large, empty calabash on the table before Sharlo.

'What would you like to eat?' asked the man, smiling.

'Anyt'ing,' answered Sharlo.

'Just say what you want,' the man explained, 'and this magic calabash will give it you. But you must say it in rhyme, like this:

'Calabash, calabash, food time come;
Bring, bring pepperpot an' gee me some.'

And so Sharlo did as the man said, and repeated the rhyme:

'Calabash, calabash, food time come;
Bring, bring pepperpot an' gee me some.'

And then like magic, hot pepperpot instantly sprang up in the calabash, filling it to the brim. Sharlo was amazed. His eyes bulged. But already his mouth was watering.

'Have a bellyful,' said the man. 'Eat your pepperpot – it's yours, all yours.' So Sharlo ate and ate, until his stomach was full and the calabash was empty. Then he licked his fingers.

The man then asked Sharlo to play the fife for him. As his stomach was full, Sharlo played even sweeter than before.

'You play wonderfully,' said the man, smiling. 'I wish I could play as sweet as you.' And he borrowed the fife and played a tune. To Sharlo's surprise the man played beautifully, though not half as sweet as he.

'A wonderful fife you have here,' said the man, rubbing his hand over the keys. 'Mmmm hmmm. A wonderful fife.'

But Sharlo was hardly listening. He was gazing at the calabash and imagining how wonderful it would be if he could have one like it, to give him all the food he wanted.

'You seem to like the calabash, Sharlo,' the man remarked.

Sharlo smiled.

'Would you like to have it?' asked the man.

Sharlo smiled again.

'Very well,' said the man, 'then we can make a bargain.'

'A bargain?' asked Sharlo, in surprise.

'Yes,' replied the man, rubbing his hand over the keys of the fife, 'a bargain that we must keep secret.'

'Wha' is de bargain?' asked Sharlo.

31

'You take my calabash,' the man explained, 'and I take your fife.'

Sharlo considered the matter for a while. He wanted the calabash, but he didn't want to part with his fife. He had had it since he was young. It was the best fife in the village. And playing it was his greatest joy – next to eating. He hesitated, unable to make up his mind.

'Come, Sharlo,' said the man, 'be sensible. You can always get another fife, but never another calabash like this again.'

'Even in hard times,' the man went on, 'this magic calabash will give you all the food you want. Think of the fungee and saltfish; the dumplings and pork; the rice and meat; the pepperpot; the souse; the ackee – all these and more are yours, all yours, just for the asking – and the eating.'

These were the very dishes Sharlo loved most. And with the calabash so near, the temptation was too great.

'All right,' he said at last, 'gimme de calabash an' tek de fife.' And so the man gave Sharlo the calabash and kept the fife.

He then led Sharlo back up the hole. The rain was over. 'Mind you, Sharlo!' said the man as they shook hands, 'keep our bargain a secret – otherwise it will be hell with me and you.' Sharlo promised to keep the bargain a secret, and they parted.

As he walked home Sharlo wondered who the strange man was. But he soon dropped the matter from his mind as he thought of the magic calabash he had got all for himself. And to test it again he said:

'Calabash, calabash, food time come;
Bring, bring ackee an' gee me some.'
And he ate the ackee all the way home.

From then onwards the calabash provided Sharlo with all the food he fancied. But from that same time he stopped cultivating his mountain lands or doing any other work. He did not get another fife, for he did not love music any more. All he now lived for was to eat.

So as the weeks passed he waxed fatter and fatter, and he

became bigger than anyone else in Glentis Village. His face was round like the dumplings he ate every day, and it became so fat that he could barely open his eyes. His body took on a barrel-like bulge, and his belly sagged over his belt like that of a pig hanging down. Six months went by, and life for Sharlo went on like this – no work, no music, and food in abundance whenever he wanted.

Then hard times struck the island. There came a long drought and life became hard for the people of Glentis Village. Many of them starved, and sometimes their only food was sugar-cane. But Sharlo's magic calabash continued to give him all he wanted. He ate more than ever, sometimes feasting like a king.

Then suddenly his dream of endless feasting ended. It happened this way. The drought had been on for three months and the villagers began to wonder where Sharlo was getting food from. For he did not go to the shops to buy anything. And his neighbours did not see him cook anything. So when he walked down the road people sometimes asked: 'But Sharlo, how you doin' so well an' we ketchin so much hell?'

This always made him laugh. And as he laughed his eyes would close, and his many chins would tremble and his belly would shake like that of a pig when it runs. But all he would say was: 'Shutmout' no ketch fly.'

So the source of his food supply remained a mystery, even to his best friends. An old friend of his named Zakky was constantly trying to find out, but Sharlo would not tell. All he would say was: 'Shut-mout' no ketch fly.'

But as the drought wore on, Zakky became desperate, for he had a wife and ten children to feed. One evening he went to see Sharlo. Sharlo was finishing a calabash of calaloo. He swallowed the last mouthful, rumbled a belch, licked his fingers, stretched his legs across the floor, and peered out of his fat, fleshy eyes at Zakky.

'Ay Sharlo,' Zakky called out, 'wha' do?'

'Ah bwoy,' Sharlo replied, 'me dey – jus' a-mek out.'

'Man you nah mekkin out,' Zakky declared, 'you fat like mud.'

33

Sharlo rumbled another belch and laughed as he clasped his fat hands across his barrel of a stomach. Zakky gazed hard at the calabash for a while and then said: 'But Sharlo, man you wort'less.'

'Wha' me do?' asked Sharlo.

'Man, you wort'less,' Zakky repeated. 'You know me an' me wife an' ten pickny an' dem a-dead fo' hungry, an' you never one time say, "Here Zakky, tek dis food fo' all-you nyam!"'

'Me food too poor fo' you,' said Sharlo.

'Too poor!' cried Zakky, 'an' de calaloo you jus' done nyam smell so nice? Man, me could nyam de calabash full o' calaloo clean right now!'

Sharlo gazed at Zakky's thin body and bony face and hollow eyes, and felt sorry for him. 'All right, Zakky', he said, 'ah givin' you some food, but you mustn' tell anybody 'bout it.' He then recited the magic rhyme:

'Calabash, calabash, food time come;
Bring, bring calaloo an' gee me some.'

Immediately the calabash became filled to the brim with hot calaloo. Zakky was amazed. He stared at the calabash with bulging eyes. At last he said, 'Well, well, well! So dis is how you gettin' food – by obeah!'

'Is not obeah,' Sharlo replied.

'Is by obeah!' Zakky repeated. 'So you become a big obeah man, eh Sharlo?'

'Is not obeah,' Sharlo repeated in defence. 'Zakky, ah tell you is not obeah.' Sharlo was afraid that Zakky would spread the word around, because it was an awful thing in Glentis Village to be called an obeah man.

'Well, if is not obeah,' said Zakky, 'wha' it is eh? Tell me, Sharlo, how else you get dis calabash full o' calaloo but by obeah?'

'All right, Zakky,' replied Sharlo, 'ah will tell you, but you mus' keep it a secret. Go ahead eat de calaloo, is good food; ah goin' tell you de story.'

Zakky began to eat the calaloo, and as he ate, Sharlo told him the whole story. When he mentioned the tall, red man,

Zakky laughed. After a while he laughed so much that he had to stop eating. By the time Sharlo had finished his story, Zakky was rocking with uncontrollable laughter, holding his sides as if they were bursting.

'Wha' mek you laugh so?' asked Sharlo.

'Is de bargain you mek wid de devil,' Zakky replied.

'De devil!' cried Sharlo, in surprise.

Zakky then explained that the tall, red man who appeared suddenly as from nowhere, and who lived in that hot place down below, and who had provided such a magic calabash, could have been no one else but the devil. It was only then that it slowly dawned on Sharlo that the man he had made the bargain with was indeed the devil.

Sharlo had always heard that it was not wise to deal with the devil, and he began to imagine what the devil had meant when he said it would be hell if the bargain was not kept a secret. He became fearful, and shuddered. He begged Zakky again and again not to tell anyone about the bargain.

Zakky promised to keep the secret. And to encourage him, Sharlo repeated the magic rhyme several times and filled a bucket of food for him to take home, and told him to return any time for more.

The next morning Zakky and his wife and their ten children went to Sharlo's home with the empty bucket for more food. They met the house open, with the front door broken off.

'Sharlo!' Zakky called.

No answer came.

Zakky and his wife and their ten children went inside.

'Sharlo!' Zakky called again, 'a whey you? A whey de calabash?'

No answer came.

They searched all over the house, and outside in the yard, and everywhere in Glentis Village, but neither Sharlo nor the calabash was anywhere to be seen.

The villagers searched for him for a long time, even in his mountain lands. But Sharlo was never seen again.

Joe's Cat

Gene Kemp

The cow parsley stood higher than his head as Joe Sprague whistled his way along the lane that led home. He carried a large bag with his cricket gear in it and he whistled because he'd just made sixty-nine runs for his team, the highest score in the last match of the year. Joe loved cricket. His dad played in the village cricket team, and Joe scored for them, and he would play for the team when he grew up. Only one thing he liked better than cricket and that was football, and soon the season would be starting and Joe in his second year at the County Comprehensive would have a good chance of playing for the second team. The school had a fine Games record and the first team were the County Champions, but Joe felt fairly sure of a place because he knew he was good. But before then, the summer holidays were nearly here, long days of helping Dad on the farm, and camping with his mates in the last week of August. And so, Joe whistled even louder as he made his way along the lane to the thatched cottage where he lived, a cottage so beautiful he did not even notice that it was.

He noticed the kitten, though.

It lay in the tufty, seeding grass that grew down the middle of the lane, where too few cars ever travelled to keep the grass down. The kitten lay so still that when Joe bent down and touched it he thought it was dead. But the thin chest moved up and down like a whisper. Joe stroked the little body very gently and the kitten stirred and rasped his hand feebly with a rough tongue. He picked it up, cradled it in one arm – it weighed as much as a leaf – picked up his bag and went on his way. He was ravenously hungry by now, and had no doubt

36

that his mother would feed the animal, as she did everything and everybody finding their way to the door.

The ham and eggs and chips and fruit pie and cream were delicious, in fact all his meals were so good that he took them for granted. He gave the kitten some milk and it slept in a corner. The other animals took no notice of it, there were so many in Joe's house that they didn't get jealous of one another but lived together with a fair amount of toleration. There was nothing wrong with the kitten, only it was very weak, as if it might have been shut away in the dark for a while with no food. No one objected to its being around. Sometimes children at school would say that they weren't allowed to have a cat or a dog or a hamster or whatever it was they fancied. Joe did not even try to understand this. A world without animals he could not imagine, it would be like a world without seasons or football and cricket.

The kitten grew fatter and stronger, and very playful. It especially liked the rabbit's foot tied to a piece of string that Joe would trail along the floor for it to pounce on, pretending it was a rat. And as it grew stronger, it grew bolder, disappearing for large parts of the day into the farmyard, but always returning for its food. It was a tom kitten, and Joe called it Boots, on account of its wide furry legs. None of the other animals bothered it much. School broke up, the holidays began and Joe at last went camping.

It was a wonderful holiday, marvellous weather, everything perfect. Only, the day Joe came home his father was killed by a tractor overturning on him at Wither's Edge, a steep field with a wooded stream in it where Joe and his mother used to picnic when he was a little boy.

There were two Joes, he sometimes thought, the Joe that had been, and now, this one who stood outside himself and watched and helped, as his mother, doing everything as carefully as ever, packed the furniture and all their things, and arranged for their successors at the cottage to have the animals, as there were none allowed in the city flat, where they were going to live to be near his mother's work. Apparently the cottage did not belong to them but had only been rented while their father had the job that went with it, and they did not have enough money to buy a house, and there were no jobs for his mother in the country. She had worked in a clothing factory before she married Joe's father, and at this she could earn enough to keep them now. She had loved the farm, running the garden and the dairy, but those days were gone.

She did not cry. Neither did Joe, and it would have been better if they had. But they were quiet people, Joe and his mother.

And it was even quieter in the flat alone all day, knowing no one, his mother out at work. Joe had never been lonely before, had not known what loneliness was. But now he knew. His mother came home almost too tired to talk. They ate their meal, silently, and went to bed.

So he was glad when school started.

Only, it was terrible.

Joe had not realised he was so slow. He'd gone, at five, to the village school, where he managed his reading and maths, and then to the County Comprehensive, where his skill at games had made him well liked and by hard work he had kept up, but here, here it was different. In a vast, dirty building surrounded by asphalt and railings, called the annexe – you went to a huge, new complex in the third and fourth year – Joe was hopelessly lost. The plan and timetable of the school were so complicated that Joe never had any idea where he was supposed to be and why. No one explained anything, and he was too shy to ask. Somehow, he just got brushed aside and submerged in enormous queues, it seemed they queued for everything. Meals, for instance; there was a choice of menu, but that choice had always gone by the time Joe arrived at the front. He couldn't quite keep up, with his work, with anything, he was always not quite ready, not quite there, he couldn't get to sleep at night and when he did, the nightmares were horrifying. He grew tall and thin instead of short and stocky. His summer tan faded.

Football. He pinned his hopes on football. He had to make a break-through with that, for it would bring fun, and with it, friendship.

The first practice was with a master with eyes and a tongue as sharp as needles. Joe didn't especially shine but he didn't make a fool of himself either. He made some useful passes, scored a goal, and found his name up on the board for another practice next day.

And he messed up the entire game. He had never played so badly in the whole of his life. Late that night, unable to sleep for thinking of it, he got up, at last, to get a drink, and as he moved about in the cramped flat, he remembered how sometimes in summer he would get up and wander about, and smell the honeysuckle and the roses, instead of the diesel fumes from the lorries roaring past, and the animals would stir and greet him lazily, rubbing round his legs.

He heard a noise. It was his mother crying for the first time. He went into her room, sat on the bed, put his arms round her and they cried together.

It was late when he awoke, for he had forgotten his alarm, and his mother had already gone to work. In the tiny kitchen with just a sink and a kitchen cabinet, so different from the kitchen at the cottage, he helped himself to cornflakes, carried them back to the living-room and bent to light the gas fire. There in front of it, fast asleep, was Boots.

Boots woke up, wrapped himself round Joe's legs, and purred with a full-blooded roar. In fact, he had grown into a pretty full-blooded cat by now, heavy and powerful, with big, furry legs. He stretched his long length up to the table, cheekily stuck his paw into the bowl of cornflakes and scooped some out. Joe didn't mind, for he had little appetite these days, so he put them on the floor, where they rapidly disappeared into Boots's tum. Then he leapt on to Joe's lap and listened attentively while Joe talked about everything, how lonely he was, how he missed his dad, how he hated seeing his mum so miserable, how he was useless at school, how he couldn't play football any more, and how he hated the city. Boots twitched an ear, and licked Joe's hand with

39

his harsh tongue. It was fairly obvious that Joe was not going to get to school that day, so after a while, Joe got dressed, raided the reserve tin money, and travelled back to his old home on the bus, accompanied by the cat.

'I'd like to keep you,' he said to it. 'But there's just no way.'

It felt strange walking up the lane with the grass growing down the middle, unreal somehow, perhaps because he'd grown so much that everything looked smaller. A youngish woman answered the door.

'What do you want?'

'I used to live here. I – I brought back the cat.'

'What cat?'

Boots had run off as soon as Joe put him down, off to investigate the farmyard, as usual.

The woman looked harassed. A few spots of rain fell.

'Come in for a minute, if you like.'

The house looked sharp and ugly to Joe. It wasn't the same place. He asked about the animals, for there were none in the kitchen.

'They're outside. I don't like them indoors. I couldn't keep track of them all.'

Upstairs a baby started to cry.

'I'll have to go, I'm sorry,' she said. 'Can I get you a cup of tea or something?'

The baby wailed even louder.

'No, thanks. I'd better go.'

A flurry of wind followed him down the lane. He looked back once or twice but could see no sign of the cat, ungrateful animal, he thought. Nearly back at home he passed a florist's and, feeling daft but determined, he bought a bunch of flowers for his mother. Once in the flat, he put them in water and began to prepare a meal.

Boots was asleep in front of the gas fire.

This time, Joe made no attempt to guess how the cat had got in. He was just there, that was all, and he wasn't taking him back again at this time of day, no thanks.

40

'My, that smells good,' said his mother, coming in, 'and those flowers, where did they come from? They're lovely.'

'Look who's here . . .' be began, but the doorbell rang; their landlady, who seemed to have taken to them.

'Now, I can't stop . . .' she was a woman who hurried all the time . . . 'downstairs tenant . . . leaving . . . flat vacant . . . from next week . . . garden . . . you'd like that . . . only a pound a week extra . . . paper round for the lad . . . know somebody . . . I'll fix it . . .'

And she was gone. Later, his mother said:

'I'll rent a TV set and make some new curtains. And if we have a garden I can plant some bulbs for the spring, and maybe we'll have an animal again, a cat perhaps?'

Boots purred with great vibration from his seat on Joe's knee.

'We can keep him then?' he asked, but his mother was reading the paper and didn't answer.

But next day, Joe had the old sick feeling again. School. School. Failure. Misery.

The first lesson was Language, which Joe used to call English in his old school. It might have a different name but what they had to do seemed familiar, write a description of a scene you know well. Joe had never been able to write descriptions, except for one he'd done of a tractor years ago, and he didn't exactly fancy that now. His hands turned to feet somehow when it came to writing, and those feet had none of the wizardry that they could sometimes – though not lately – show on the field.

But as he sat there something wrapped round his legs under the table. He shot down a hand, a furry face rubbed against it and a harsh tongue licked it. Good Lord, Boots was here. That cat had a genius for getting into places. Well, they'd better both keep quiet, or there would be trouble. He looked round furtively. No one appeared to have noticed anything. Best thing was to start writing and pray that Boots sat quietly till mid-morning. Joe picked up his pen, and the sights and smells and sounds of the farmyard came to him so vividly that the words flowed out of his head and poured down the page. He had never in his life written like that. The buzzer, usually so long and anxiously awaited, rang before he'd finished.

'Can I go on with it later?' he asked the teacher. He noticed in surprise that she had a kind and pleasant face.

'Miss Downes,' she prompted, smiling. 'Of course you can. And oh, Joe, do come and see me if you are worried about anything.'

He'd got outside before he remembered Boots, but when he returned to the classroom there was no sign of the cat anywhere. A West Indian girl stood by the door, very pretty, and laughing. She terrified him, he was always shy of girls, and the girls in this class seemed so sharp and clever and shiny, somehow. Then she stopped laughing and smiled at him, instead.

'Come with us, and we'll show you around. Reckon you might need a bit of looking after.'

Suddenly he was surrounded by three of them and scared out of his wits, but then a boy appeared out of nowhere, a boy he'd noticed before and liked, a boy who was very nippy with a football.

Together they all made their way into the playground.

Joe found his name on the practice list again. And this time he was determined to do well. He had friends now, lots of them, but especially Mark, the footballer, and Davina the girl who had spoken to him first. He felt happy and confident as he ran on to the pitch.

Yet some of his old skill had left him, try as he might, and after ten minutes or so, a wave of such misery swept over him that he felt like running off the pitch and leaving everything. And out of the blue, through the tears that blurred his sight, a furry figure appeared, standing on bulky back legs, and, trapping the ball in them, he sent it direct to Joe, who scored a superb goal. Next day his name went up among the team.

He walked home with Mark and Davina. When he got in Boots was asleep in front of the fire. He woke, stretched right up to the table on his big back legs, licked Joe's face with his sandpaper tongue, and vanished. Joe searched and called but he was nowhere to be found.

When he asked his mother about him, she said she'd never seen the cat, either at the farm or the flat.

Joe never saw him again.

Only, sometimes, when things grew difficult or he was unhappy, it would seem that he would feel the fleeting rasp of a sandpaper tongue on his hand and the flourish of a bushy tail around his legs.

Lenny's Red-Letter Day

Bernard Ashley

Lenny Fraser is a boy in my class. Well, he's a boy in my class when he comes. But to tell the truth, he doesn't come very often. He stays away from school for a week at a time, and I'll tell you where he is. He's at the shops, stealing things sometimes, but mainly just opening the doors for people. He does it to keep himself warm. I've seen him in our shop. When he opens the door for someone, he stands around inside till he gets sent out. Of course, it's quite warm enough in school, but he hates coming. He's always got long tangled hair, not very clean, and his clothes are too big or too small, and they call him 'Flea-bag'. He sits at a desk without a partner, and no one wants to hold his hand in games. All right, they're not to blame; but he isn't, either. His mother never gets up in the morning, and his house is dirty. It's a house that everybody runs past very quickly.

But Lenny makes me laugh a lot. In the playground he's always saying funny things out of the corner of his mouth. He doesn't smile when he does it. He says these funny things as if he's complaining. For example, when Mr Cox the deputy head came to school in his new car, Lenny came too, that day; but he didn't join in all the admiration. He looked at the little car and said to me, 'Anyone missing a skate-board?'

He misses all the really good things, though – the School Journeys and the outing. And it was a big shame about his birthday.

44

It happens like this with birthdays in our class. Miss Blake lets everyone bring their cards and perhaps a small present to show the others. Then everyone sings 'Happy Birthday' and we give them bumps in the playground. If people can't bring a present, they tell everyone what they've got instead. I happen to know some people make up the things that they've got just to be up with the others, but Miss Blake says it's good to share our Red-Letter Days.

I didn't know about these Red-Letter Days before. I thought they were something special in the post, like my dad handles in his Post Office in the shop. But Miss Blake told us they are red printed words in the prayer books, meaning special days.

Well, what I'm telling you is that Lenny came to school on his birthday this year. Of course, he didn't tell us it was his birthday, and, as it all worked out, it would have been better if Miss Blake hadn't noticed it in the register. But, 'How nice!' she said. 'Lenny's here on his birthday, and we can share it with him.'

It wasn't very nice for Lenny. He didn't have any cards to show the class, and he couldn't think of a birthday present to tell us about. He couldn't even think of anything funny to say out of the corner of his mouth. He just had to stand there looking foolish until Miss Blake started the singing of 'Happy Birthday' – and then half the people didn't bother to sing it. I felt very sorry for him, I can tell you. But that wasn't the worst. The worst happened in the playground. I went to take his head end for bumps, and no one would come and take his feet. They all walked away. I had to finish up just patting him on the head with my hands, and before I knew what was coming out I was telling him, 'You can come home to tea with me, for your birthday.' And he said, yes, he would come.

My father works very hard in the Post Office, in a corner of our shop; and my mother stands at the door all day, where people pay for their groceries. When I get home from school, I carry cardboard boxes out to the yard and jump on them, or my big sister Nalini shows me which shelves to fill and I fill

45

them with jam or chapatis – or birthday cards. On this day, though, I thought I'd use my key and go in through the side door and take Lenny straight upstairs – then hurry down again and tell my mum and dad that I'd got a friend in for an hour. I thought, I can get a birthday card and some cake and ice-cream from the shop, and Lenny can go home before they come upstairs. I wanted him to do that before my dad saw who it was, because he knows Lenny from his hanging around the shops.

Lenny said some funny things on the way home from school, but you know, I couldn't relax and enjoy them properly. I felt ashamed because I was wishing all the time that I hadn't asked him to come home with me. The bottoms of his trousers dragged along the ground, he had no buttons on his shirt so the sleeves flapped, and his hair must have made it hard for him to see where he was going.

I was in luck because the shop was very busy. My dad had a queue of people to pay out, and my mum had a crowd at the till. I left Lenny in the living-room and I went down to get what I wanted from the shop. I found him a birthday card with a badge in it. When I came back, he was sitting in a chair and the television was switched on. He's a good one at helping himself, I thought. We watched some cartoons and then we played 'Monopoly', which Lenny had seen on the shelf. We had some crisps and cakes and lemonade while we were playing; but I had only one eye on my 'Monopoly' moves – the other eye was on the clock all the time. I was getting very impatient for the game to finish, because it looked as if Lenny would still be there when they came up from the shop. I did some really bad moves so that I could lose quickly, but it's very difficult to hurry up 'Monopoly', as you may know.

In the end I did such stupid things – like buying too many houses and selling Park Lane and Mayfair – that he won the game. He must have noticed what I was doing, but he didn't say anything to me. Hurriedly, I gave him his birthday card. He pretended not to take very much notice of it, but he put it in his shirt, and kept feeling it to make sure it was still there.

At least, that's what I thought he was making sure about, there inside his shirt.

It was just the right time to say goodbye, and I'm just thinking he can go without anyone seeing him, when my sister came in. She had run up from the shop for something or other, and she put her head inside the room. At some other time, I would have laughed out loud at her stupid face. When she saw Lenny, she looked as if she'd opened the door and seen something really unpleasant. I could gladly have given her a good kick. She shut the door a lot quicker than she opened it, and I felt really bad about it.

'Nice to meet you,' Lenny joked, but his face said he wanted to go, too, and I wasn't going to be the one to stop him.

I let him out, and I heaved a big sigh. I felt good about being kind to him, the way you do when you've done a sponsored swim, and I'd done it without my mum and dad frowning at me about who I brought home. Only Nalini had seen him, and everyone knows she can make things seem worse than they are. I washed the glasses, and I can remember singing while I stood at the sink. I was feeling very pleased with myself.

My good feeling lasted about fifteen minutes; just long enough to be wearing off slightly. Then Nalini came in again and destroyed it altogether.

'Prakash, have you seen that envelope that was on the television top?' she asked. 'I put it on here when I came in from school.'

'No,' I said. It was very soon to be getting worried, but things inside me were turning over like clothes in a washing-machine. I knew already where all this was going to end up. 'What was in it?' My voice sounded to me as if it was coming from a great distance.

She was looking everywhere in the room, but she kept coming back to the television top as if the envelope would mysteriously appear there. She stood there now, staring at me. '*What was in it?* What was in it was only a Postal Order for five pounds! Money for my school trip!'

47

'What does it look like?' I asked, but I think we both knew that I was only stalling. We both knew where it had gone.

'It's a white piece of paper in a brown envelope. It says "Postal Order" on it, in red.'

My washing-machine inside nearly went into a fast spin when I heard that. It was certainly Lenny's Red-Letter Day! But how could he be so ungrateful, I thought, when I was the only one to be kind to him? I clenched my fist while I pretended to look around. I wanted to punch him hard on the nose.

Then Nalini said what was in both our minds. 'It's that dirty kid who's got it. I'm going down to tell Dad. I don't know what makes you so stupid.'

Right at that moment I didn't know what made me so stupid, either, as to leave him up there on his own. I should have known. Didn't Miss Banks once say something about leopards never changing their spots?

When the shop closed, there was an awful business in the room. My dad was shouting-angry at me, and my mum couldn't think of anything good to say.

'You know where this boy lives,' my dad said. 'Tell me now, while I telephone the police. There's only one way of dealing with this sort of thing. If I go up there, I shall only get a mouthful of abuse. As if it isn't bad enough for you to see me losing things out of the shop, you have to bring untrustworthy people upstairs!'

My mum saw how unhappy I was, and she tried to make things better. 'Can't you cancel the Postal Order?' she asked him.

'Of course not. Even if he hasn't had the time to cash it somewhere else by now, how long do you think the Post Office would let me be Sub-Postmaster if I did that sort of thing?'

I was feeling very bad for all of us, but the thought of the police calling at Lenny's house was making me feel worse.

'I'll get it back,' I said. 'I'll go to his house. It's only along the road from the school. And if I don't get it back, I can get the exact number of where he lives. *Then* you can telephone the police.' I had never spoken to my dad like that before, but I was feeling all shaky inside, and all the world seemed a different place to me that evening. I didn't give anybody a chance to argue with me. I ran straight out of the room and down to the street.

My secret hopes of seeing Lenny before I got to his house didn't come to anything. All too quickly I was there, pushing back his broken gate and walking up the cracked path to his front door. There wasn't a door knocker. I flapped the letter-box, and I started to think my dad was right. The police would have been better doing this than me.

I had never seen his mother before, only heard about her from other kids who lived near. When she opened the door, I could see she was a small lady with a tight mouth and eyes that said, 'Who are you?' and 'Go away from here!' at the same time.

She opened the door only a little bit, ready to slam it on me. I had to be quick.

'Is Lenny in, please?' I asked her.

She said, 'What's it to you?'

'He's a friend of mine,' I told her. 'Can I see him, please?'

She made a face as if she had something nasty in her mouth. 'LENNY!' she shouted. 'COME HERE!'

Lenny came slinking down the passage, like one of those scared animals in a circus. He kept his eyes on her hands, once he'd seen who it was at the door. There weren't any funny remarks coming from him.

She jerked her head at me. 'How many times have I told you not to bring kids to the house?' she shouted at him. She made it sound as if she was accusing him of a bad crime.

Lenny had nothing to say. She was hanging over him like a vulture about to fix its talons into a rabbit. It looked so out of place it didn't seem real. Then it came to me that it could be play-acting – the two of them. He had given her the five pounds, and she was putting this on to get rid of me quickly.

But suddenly she slammed the door so hard in my face I could see how the glass in it came to be broken.

'Well, I don't want kinds coming to my door!' she shouted

49

at him on the other side. 'Breaking the gate, breaking the windows, wearing out the path. How can I keep this place nice when I'm forever dragging to the door?'

She hit him then, I know she did. There was no play-acting about the bang as a foot hit the door, and Lenny yelling out loud as if a desk lid had come down on his head. But I didn't stop to hear any more. I'd heard enough to turn my stomach sick. Poor Lenny – I'd been worried about my mum and dad seeing him – and look what happened when his mother saw me! She had to be mad, that woman. And Lenny had to live with her! I didn't feel like crying, although my eyes had a hot rawness in them. More than anything, I just wanted to be back at home with my own family and the door shut tight.

Seeing my dad's car turn the corner was as if my dearest wish had been granted. He was going slowly, searching for me, with Nalini sitting up in front with big eyes. I waved, and ran to them. I got in the back and I drew in my breath to tell them to go straight home. It was worth fifty pounds not to have them knocking at Lenny's house, never mind five. But they were too busy trying to speak to me.

'Have you been to the house? Did you say anything?'

'Yes, I've been to the house, but –'

'Did you accuse him?'

'No. I didn't have a chance –'

They both sat back in their seats, as if the car would drive itself home.

'Well, we must be grateful for that.'

'We found the Postal Order.'

I could hardly believe what my ears were hearing. *They had found the Postal Order.* Lenny hadn't taken it, after all!

'It wasn't in its envelope,' Nalini was saying. 'He must have taken it out of that when he was tempted by it. But we can't accuse him of screwing up an envelope and hiding it in his pocket.'

'No, no,' I was saying, urging her to get on with things and tell me. 'So where was it?'

'In with the "Monopoly" money. He couldn't put it back

50

on the television, so he must have kept it in his pile of "Monopoly" money, and put it back in the box.'

'Oh.'

'Mum found it. In all the commotion after you went out she knocked the box off the chair, and when she picked the bits up, there was the Postal Order.'

'It's certainly a good job you said nothing about it,' my dad said. 'And a good job I didn't telephone the police. We should have looked very small.'

All I could think was how small I had just felt, standing at Lenny's slammed door and hearing what his mother had said to him. And what about him getting beaten for having a friend call at his house?

My dad tried to be cheerful. 'Anyway, who won?' he asked.

'Lenny won the "Monopoly",' I said.

In bed that night, I lay awake a long time, thinking about it all. Lenny had taken some hard punishment from his mother. Some Red-Letter Day it had turned out to be! He would bear some hard thoughts about Prakash Patel.

He didn't come to school for a long time after that. But when he did, my heart sank into my boots. He came straight across the playground, the same flappy sleeves and dragging trouser bottoms, the same long, tangled hair – and he came straight for me. What would he do? Hit me? Spit in my face?

As he got close, I saw what was on his shirt, pinned there like a medal. It was his birthday badge.

'It's a good game, that "Monopoly",' he said out of the corner of his mouth. It was as if he was trying to tell me something.

'Yes,' I said. 'It's a good game all right.'

I hadn't got the guts to tell him that I'd gone straight home that night and thrown it in the dustbin. Dealings with houses didn't appeal to me any more.

The Hitch-hiker

Roald Dahl

I had a new car. It was an exciting toy, a big BMW 3.3 Li,
which means 3.3 litre, long wheelbase, fuel injection. It had
a top speed of 129 m.p.h. and terrific acceleration. The body
was pale blue. The seats inside were darker blue and they
were made of leather, genuine soft leather of the finest
quality. The windows were electrically operated and so was
the sun-roof. The radio aerial popped up when I switched on
the radio, and disappeared when I switched it off. The
powerful engine growled and grunted impatiently at slow
speeds, but at sixty miles an hour the growling stopped and
the motor began to purr with pleasure.

I was driving up to London by myself. It was a lovely June
day. They were haymaking in the fields and there were
buttercups along both sides of the road. I was whispering
along at seventy miles an hour, leaning back comfortably in
my seat, with no more than a couple of fingers resting lightly
on the wheel to keep her steady. Ahead of me I saw a man
thumbing a lift. I touched the footbrake and brought the car
to a stop beside him. I always stopped for hitch-hikers. I
knew just how it used to feel to be standing on the side of a
country road watching the cars go by. I hated the drivers for
pretending they didn't see me, especially the ones in big cars
with three empty seats. The large expensive cars seldom
stopped. It was always the smaller ones that offered you a
lift, or the old rusty ones, or the ones that were already
crammed full of children and the driver would say, 'I think
we can squeeze in one more.'

The hitch-hiker poked his head through the open window
and said, 'Going to London, guv'nor?'

'Yes,' I said. 'Jump in.'

He got in and I drove on.

He was a small ratty-faced man with grey teeth. His eyes were dark and quick and clever, like a rat's eyes, and his ears were slightly pointed at the top. He had a cloth cap on his head and he was wearing a greyish-coloured jacket with enormous pockets. The grey jacket, together with the quick eyes and the pointed ears, made him look more than anything like some sort of a huge human rat.

'What part of London are you headed for?' I asked him.

'I'm goin' right through London and out the other side,' he said. 'I'm goin' to Epsom, for the races. It's Derby Day today.'

'So it is,' I said. 'I wish I were going with you. I love betting on horses.'

'I never bet on horses,' he said. 'I don't even watch 'em run. That's a stupid silly business.'

'Then why do you go?' I asked.

He didn't seem to like that question. His little ratty face went absolutely blank and he sat there staring straight ahead at the road, saying nothing.

'I expect you help to work the betting machines or something like that,' I said.

'That's even sillier,' he answered. 'There's no fun working them lousy machines and selling tickets to mugs. Any fool could do that.'

There was a long silence. I decided not to question him any more. I remembered how irritated I used to get in my hitch-hiking days when drivers kept asking *me* questions. Where are you going? Why are you going there? What's your job? Are you married? Do you have a girl-friend? What's her name? How old are you? And so on and so forth. I used to hate it.

'I'm sorry,' I said. 'It's none of my business what you do. The trouble is, I'm a writer, and most writers are terrible nosey parkers.'

'You write books?' he asked.

'Yes.'

'Writin' books is okay,' he said. 'It's what I call a skilled trade. I'm in a skilled trade too. The folks I despise is them that spend all their lives doin' crummy old routine jobs with no skill in 'em at all. You see what I mean?'

'Yes.'

'The secret of life,' he said, 'is to become very very good at somethin' that's very very 'ard to do.'

'Like you,' I said.

'Exactly. You and me both.'

'What makes you think that *I'm* any good at my job?' I asked. 'There's an awful lot of bad writers around.'

'You wouldn't be drivin' about in a car like this if you weren't no good at it,' he answered. 'It must've cost a tidy packet, this little job.'

'It wasn't cheap.'

'What can she do flat out?' he asked.

'One hundred and twenty-nine miles an hour,' I told him.

'I'll bet she won't do it.'

'I'll bet she will.'

'All car makers is liars,' he said. 'You can buy any car you like and it'll never do what the makers say it will in the ads.'

'This one will.'

'Open 'er up then and prove it,' he said. 'Go on, guv'nor, open 'er right up and let's see what she'll do.'

There is a roundabout at Chalfont St Peter and immediately beyond it there's a long straight section of dual carriage-way. We came out of the roundabout on to the carriage-way and I pressed my foot hard down on the accelerator. The big car leaped forward as though she'd been stung. In ten seconds or so, we were doing ninety.

'Lovely!' he cried. 'Beautiful! Keep goin'!'

I had the accelerator jammed right down against the floor and I held it there.

'One hundred!' he shouted . . . 'A hundred and five! . . . A hundred and ten! . . . A hundred and fifteen! Go on! Don't slack off!'

I was in the outside lane and we flashed past several cars as

54

though they were standing still – a green Mini, a big cream-coloured Citroën, a white Land-Rover, a huge truck with a container on the back, an orange-coloured Volkswagen Minibus . . .

'A hundred and twenty!' my passenger shouted, jumping up and down. 'Go on! Go on! Get 'er up to one-two-nine!'

At that moment, I heard the scream of a police siren. It was so loud it seemed to be right inside the car, and then a policeman on a motor-cycle loomed up alongside us on the inside lane and went past us and raised a hand for us to stop.

'Oh, my sainted aunt!' I said. 'That's torn it!'

The policeman must have been doing about a hundred and thirty when he passed us, and he took plenty of time slowing down. Finally, he pulled into the side of the road and I pulled in behind him. 'I didn't know police motor-cycles could go as fast as that,' I said rather lamely.

'That one can,' my passenger said. 'It's the same make as yours. It's a BMW R90S. Fastest bike on the road. That's what they're usin' nowadays.'

The policeman got off his motor-cycle and leaned the machine sideways on to its prop stand. Then he took off his gloves and placed them carefully on the seat. He was in no hurry now. He had us where he wanted us and he knew it.

'This is real trouble,' I said. 'I don't like it one bit.'

'Don't talk to 'im any more than is necessary, you understand,' my companion said. 'Just sit tight and keep mum.'

Like an executioner approaching his victim, the policeman came strolling slowly towards us. He was a big meaty man with a belly, and his blue breeches were skin-tight around his enormous thighs. His goggles were pulled up on to the helmet, showing a smouldering red face with wide cheeks.

We sat there like guilty schoolboys, waiting for him to arrive.

'Watch out for this man,' my passenger whispered. ' 'Ee looks mean as the devil.'

The policeman came round to my open window and placed one meaty hand on the sill. 'What's the hurry?' he said.

'No hurry, officer,' I answered.

'Perhaps there's a woman in the back having a baby and you're rushing her to hospital? Is that it?'

'No, officer.'

'Or perhaps your house is on fire and you're dashing home to rescue the family from upstairs?' His voice was dangerously soft and mocking.

'My house isn't on fire, officer.'

'In that case,' he said, 'you've got yourself into a nasty mess, haven't you? Do you know what the speed limit is in this country?'

'Seventy,' I said.

'And do you mind telling me exactly what speed you were doing just now?'

I shrugged and didn't say anything.

When he spoke next, he raised his voice so loud that I jumped. *'One hundred and twenty miles per hour!'* he barked. 'That's *fifty* miles an hour over the limit!'

He turned his head and spat out a big gob of spit. It landed on the wing of my car and started sliding down over my beautiful blue paint. Then he turned back again and stared hard at my passenger. 'And who are you?' he asked sharply.

'He's a hitch-hiker,' I said. 'I'm giving him a lift.'

'I didn't ask you,' he said. 'I asked him.'

' 'Ave I done somethin' wrong?' my passenger asked. His voice was as soft and oily as haircream.

'That's more than likely,' the policeman answered. 'Anyway, you're a witness. I'll deal with you in a minute. Driving licence,' he snapped, holding out his hand.

I gave him my driving-licence.

He unbuttoned the left-hand breast-pocket of his tunic and brought out the dreaded book of tickets. Carefully he copied the name and address from my licence. Then he gave it back to me. He strolled round to the front of the car and read the number from the number-plate and wrote that down as well. He filled in the date, the time and the details of my offence. Then he tore out the top copy of the ticket. But before handing it to me, he checked that all the information had come through clearly on his own carbon copy. Finally, he replaced the book in his tunic pocket and fastened the button.

'Now you,' he said to my passenger, and he walked around to the other side of the car. From the other breast-pocket he produced a small black notebook. 'Name?' he snapped.

'Michael Fish,' my passenger said.

'Address?'

'Fourteen, Windsor Lane, Luton.'

'Show me something to prove this is your real name and address,' the policeman said.

My passenger fished in his pockets and came out with a driving-licence of his own. The policeman checked the name and address and handed it back to him. 'What's your job?' he asked sharply.

'I'm an 'od carrier.'

'A *what*?'

'An 'od carrier.'

'Spell it.'

'H-O-D-C-A- . . .'

'That'll do. And what's a hod carrier, may I ask?'

'An 'od carrier, officer, is a person 'oo carries the cement up the ladder to the bricklayer. And the 'od is what 'ee carries it in. It's got a long 'andle, and on the top you've got two bits of wood set at an angle . . .'

'All right, all right. Who's your employer?'

'Don't 'ave one. I'm unemployed.'

The policeman wrote all this down in the black notebook. Then he returned the book to its pocket and did up the button.

'When I get back to the station I'm going to do a little checking up on you,' he said to my passenger.

'Me? What've I done wrong?' the rat-faced man asked.

'I don't like your face, that's all,' the policeman said. 'And we just might have a picture of it somewhere in our files.' He strolled round the car and returned to my window.

'I suppose you know you're in serious trouble,' he said to me.

'Yes, officer.'

'You won't be driving this fancy car of yours again for a very long time, not after *we've* finished with you. You won't be driving *any* car again come to that for several years. And a good thing, too. I hope they lock you up for a spell into the bargain.'

'You mean prison?' I asked, alarmed.

'Absolutely,' he said, smacking his lips. 'In the clink. Behind the bars. Along with all the other criminals who break the law. *And* a hefty fine into the bargain. Nobody will be more pleased about that than me. I'll see you in court, both of you. You'll be getting a summons to appear.'

He turned away and walked over to his motor-cycle. He flipped the prop stand back into position with his foot and swung his leg over the saddle. Then he kicked the starter and roared off up the road out of sight.

'Phew!' I gasped. 'That's done it.'

'We was caught,' my passenger said. 'We was caught good and proper.'

'I was caught, you mean.'

'That's right,' he said. 'What you goin' to do now, guv'nor?'

'I'm going straight up to London to talk to my solicitor,' I said. I started the car and drove on.

'You mustn't believe what 'ee said to you about goin' to prison,' my passenger said. 'They don't put nobody in the clink just for speedin'.'

'Are you sure of that?' I asked.

'I'm positive,' he answered. 'They can take your licence away and they can give you a whoppin' big fine, but that'll be the end of it.'

I felt tremendously relieved.

'By the way,' I said, 'why did you lie to him?'

'Who, me?' he said. 'What makes you think I lied?'

'You told him you were an unemployed hod carrier. But you told *me* you were in a highly skilled trade.'

'So I am,' he said. 'But it don't pay to tell everythin' to a copper.'

58

'So what *do* you do?' I asked him.

'Ah,' he said slyly. 'That'd be tellin', wouldn't it?'

'Is it something you're ashamed of?'

'Ashamed?' he cried. 'Me, ashamed of my job? I'm about as proud of it as anybody could be in the entire world!'

'Then why won't you tell me?'

'You writers really is nosey parkers, aren't you?' he said. 'And you ain't goin' to he 'appy, I don't think, until you've found out exactly what the answer is?'

'I don't really care one way or the other,' I told him, lying.

He gave me a crafty little ratty look out of the sides of his eyes. 'I think you do care,' he said. 'I can see it on your face that you think I'm in some kind of a very peculiar trade and you're just achin' to know what it is.'

I didn't like the way he read my thoughts. I kept quiet and stared at the road ahead.

'You'd be right, too,' he went on. 'I *am* in a very peculiar trade. I'm in the queerest peculiar trade of 'em all.'

I waited for him to go on.

'That's why I 'as to be extra careful 'oo I'm talkin' to, you see. 'Ow am I to know, for instance, you're not another copper in plain clothes?'

'Do I look like a copper?'

'No,' he said. 'You don't. And you ain't. Any fool could tell that.'

He took from his pocket a tin of tobacco and a packet of cigarette papers and started to roll a cigarette. I was watching him out of the corner of one eye, and the speed with which he performed this rather difficult operation was incredible. The cigarette was rolled and ready in about five seconds. He ran his tongue along the edge of the paper, stuck it down and popped the cigarette between his lips. Then, as if from nowhere, a lighter appeared in his hand. The lighter flamed. The cigarette was lit. The lighter disappeared. It was altogether a remarkable performance.

'I've never seen anyone roll a cigarette as fast as that,' I said.

'Ah,' he said, taking a deep suck of smoke. 'So you noticed.'

'Of course I noticed. It was quite fantastic.'

He sat back and smiled. It pleased him very much that I had noticed how quickly he could roll a cigarette. 'You want to know what makes me able to do it?' he asked.

'Go on then.'

'It's because I've got fantastic fingers. These fingers of mine,' he said, holding up both hands high in front of him, 'are quicker and cleverer than the fingers of the best piano player in the world!'

'Are you a piano player?'

'Don't be daft,' he said. 'Do I look like a piano player?'

I glanced at his fingers. They were so beautifully shaped, so slim and long and elegant, they didn't seem to belong to the rest of him at all. They looked more like the fingers of a brain surgeon or a watchmaker.

'My job', he went on, 'is a hundred times more difficult than playin' the piano. Any twerp can learn to do that. There's titchy little kids learnin' to play the piano in almost any 'ouse you go into these days. That's right, ain't it?'

'More or less,' I said.

'Of course it's right. But there's not one person in ten million can learn to do what I do. Not one in ten million! 'Ow about that?'

'Amazing,' I said.

'You're darn right it's amazin',' he said.

'I think I know what you do,' I said. 'You do conjuring tricks. You're a conjurer.'

'Me?' he snorted. 'A conjurer? Can you picture me goin' round crummy kids' parties makin' rabbits come out of top 'ats?'

'Then you're a card player. You get people into card games and you deal yourself marvellous hands.'

'Me! A rotten card-sharper!' he cried. 'That's a miserable racket if ever there was one.'

'All right. I give up.'

I was taking the car along slowly now, at no more than

60

forty miles an hour, to make quite sure I wasn't stopped again. We had come on to the main London–Oxford road and were running down the hill toward Denham.

Suddenly, my passenger was holding up a black leather belt in his hand. 'Ever seen this before?' he asked. The belt had a brass buckle of unusual design.

'Hey!' I said. 'That's mine, isn't it? It *is* mine! Where did you get it?'

He grinned and waved the belt gently from side to side. 'Where d'you think I got it?' he said. 'Off the top of your trousers, of course.'

I reached down and felt for my belt. It was gone.

'You mean you took it off me while we've been driving along?' I asked, flabbergasted.

He nodded, watching me all the time with those little black ratty eyes.

'That's impossible,' I said. 'You'd have had to undo the buckle and slide the whole thing out through the loops all the way round. I'd have seen you doing it. And even if I hadn't seen you, I'd have felt it.'

'Ah, but you didn't, did you?' he said, triumphant. He dropped the belt on his lap, and now all at once there was a brown shoelace dangling from his fingers. 'And what about this, then?' he exclaimed, waving the shoelace.

'What about it?' I said.

'Anyone around 'ere missin' a shoelace?' he asked, grinning.

I glanced down at my shoes. The lace of one of them was missing. 'Good grief!' I said. 'How did you do that? I never saw you bending down.'

'You never saw nothin',' he said proudly. 'You never even saw me move an inch. And you know why?'

'Yes,' I said. 'Because you've got fantastic fingers.'

'Exactly right!' he cried. 'You catch on pretty quick, don't you?' He sat back and sucked away at his home-made cigarette, blowing the smoke out in a thin stream against the windshield. He knew he had impressed me greatly with those two tricks, and this made him very happy. 'I don't want to be late,' he said. 'What time is it?'

'There's a clock in front of you,' I told him.

'I don't trust car clocks,' he said. 'What does your watch say?'

I hitched up my sleeve to look at the watch on my wrist. It wasn't there. I looked at the man. He looked back at me, grinning.

'You've taken that, too,' I said.

He held out his hand and there was my watch lying on his palm. 'Nice bit of stuff, this,' he said. 'Superior quality. Eighteen-carat gold. Easy to flog, too. It's never any trouble gettin' rid of quality goods.'

'I'd like it back, if you don't mind,' I said rather huffily.

He placed the watch carefully on the leather tray in front of him. 'I wouldn't nick anything from you, guv'nor,' he said. 'You're my pal. You're givin' me a lift.'

'I'm glad to hear it,' I said.

'All I'm doin' is answerin' your question,' he went on. 'You asked me what I did for a livin' and I'm showin' you.'

'What else have you got of mine?'

He smiled again, and now he started to take from the pocket of his jacket one thing after another that belonged to me – my driving-licence, a key-ring with four keys on it, some pound notes, a few coins, a letter from my publishers, my diary, a stubby old pencil, a cigarette-lighter, and last of all, a beautiful old sapphire ring with pearls around it belonging to my wife. I was taking the ring up to the jeweller in London because one of the pearls was missing.

'Now *there's* another lovely piece of goods,' he said, turning the ring over in his fingers. 'That's eighteenth century, if I'm not mistaken, from the reign of King George the Third.'

'You're right,' I said, impressed. 'You're absolutely right.'

He put the ring on the leather tray with the other items.

'So you're a pickpocket,' I said.

'I don't like that word,' he answered. 'It's a coarse and vulgar word. Pickpockets is coarse and vulgar people who only do easy little amateur jobs. They lift money from blind old ladies.'

'What do you call yourself, then?'

'Me? I'm a fingersmith. I'm a professional fingersmith.' He spoke the words solemnly and proudly, as though he were telling me he was the President of the Royal College of Surgeons or the Archbishop of Canterbury.

'I've never heard that word before,' I said. 'Did you invent it?'

'Of course I didn't invent it,' he replied. 'It's the name given to them who's risen to the very top of the profession. You've 'eard of a goldsmith and a silversmith, for instance. They're experts with gold and silver. I'm an expert with my fingers, so I'm a fingersmith.'

'It must be an interesting job.'

'It's a marvellous job,' he answered. 'It's lovely.'

'And that's why you go to the races?'

'Race meetings is easy meat,' he said. 'You just stand around after the race, watchin' for the lucky ones to queue up and draw their money. And when you see someone collectin' a big bundle of notes, you simply follows after 'im and 'elps yourself. But don't get me wrong, guv'nor. I never takes nothin' from a loser. Nor from poor people neither. I only go after them as can afford it, the winners and the rich.'

'That's very thoughtful of you,' I said. 'How often do you get caught?'

'Caught?' he cried, disgusted. '*Me* get caught! It's only pickpockets get caught. Fingersmiths never. Listen, I could take the false teeth out of your mouth if I wanted to and you wouldn't even catch me!'

'I don't have false teeth,' I said.

'I know you don't,' he answered. 'Otherwise I'd 'ave 'ad 'em out long ago!'

I believed him. Those long slim fingers of his seemed able to do anything.

We drove on for a while without talking.

'That policeman's going to check up on you pretty thoroughly,' I said. 'Doesn't that worry you a bit?'

'Nobody's checkin' up on me,' he said.

'Of course they are. He's got your name and address written down most carefully in his black book.'

The man gave me another of his sly, ratty little smiles. 'Ah,' he said. 'So 'ee 'as. But I'll bet 'ee ain't got it all written down in 'is memory as well. I've never known a copper yet with a decent memory. Some of 'em can't even remember their own names.'

'What's memory got to do with it?' I asked. 'It's written down in his book, isn't it?'

'Yes, guv'nor, it is. But the trouble is, 'ee's lost the book. ' 'Ee's lost both books, the one with my name in it *and* the one with yours.'

In the long delicate fingers of his right hand, the man was holding up in triumph the two books he had taken from the policeman's pockets. 'Easiest job I ever done,' he announced proudly.

I nearly swerved the car into a milk-truck, I was so excited.

'That copper's got nothing on either of us now,' he said.

'You're a genius!' I cried.

' 'Ee's got no names, no addresses, no car number, no nothin' ' he said.

'You're brilliant!'

'I think you'd better pull in off this main road as soon as possible', he said. 'Then we'd better build a little bonfire and burn these books.'

'You're a fantastic fellow,' I exclaimed.

'Thank you, guv'nor,' he said. 'It's always nice to be appreciated.'

The Choice
Is Yours

Jan Mark

The Music Room was on one side of the quadrangle and the
Changing Room faced it on the other. They were linked by a
corridor that made up the third side, and the fourth was the
view across the playing-fields. In the Music Room Miss
Helen Francis sat at the piano, head bent over the keyboard
as her fingers tittuped from note to note, and swaying back
and forth like a snake charming itself. At the top of the
Changing Room steps Miss Marion Taylor stood, sportively
poised with one hand on the doorknob and a whistle dangling on a string from the other; quivering with eagerness to
be out on the field and inhaling fresh air. They could see each
other. Brenda, standing in the doorway of the Music Room,
could see them both.

'Well, come in, child,' said Miss Francis. 'Don't *haver*. If
you must haver, don't do it in the doorway. Other people are
trying to come in.'

Brenda moved to one side to make way for the other
people, members of the choir who would normally have
shoved her out of the way and pushed past. Here they shed
their school manners in the corridor and queued in attitudes
of excruciated patience. Miss Helen Francis favoured the
noiseless approach. Across the quadrangle the Under-
Thirteen Hockey XI roistered, and Miss Marion Taylor
failed to intervene. Miss Francis observed all this with misty
disapproval and looked away again.

'Brenda dear, are you coming in, or going out, or putting down roots?'

The rest of the choir was by now seated; first sopranos on the right, second sopranos on the left, thirds across one end and Miss Humphry, who was billed as an alto but sang tenor, at the other. They all sat up straight, as trained by Miss Francis, and looked curiously at Brenda who should have been seated too, among the first sopranos. Her empty chair was in the front row, with the music stacked on it, all ready. Miss Francis cocked her head to one side like a budgerigar that sees a millet spray in the offing.

'Have you a message for us, dear? From above?' She meant the headmistress, but by her tone it could have been God and his angels.

'No, Miss Francis.'

'From *beyond*?'

'Miss Francis, can I ask – ?'

'You *may* ask, Brenda. Whether or not you *can* is beyond my powers of divination.'

Brenda saw that the time for havering was at an end.

'Please, Miss Francis, may I be excused from choir?'

The budgie instantly turned into a marabou stork.

'Excused, Brenda? Do you have a pain?'

'There's a hockey practice, Miss Francis.'

'I am aware of that.' Miss Francis cast a look, over her shoulder and across the quadrangle, that should have turned Miss Taylor to stone, and the Under-Thirteen XI with her. 'How does it concern you, Brenda? How does it concern me?'

'I'm in the team, Miss Francis, and there's a match on Saturday,' said Brenda.

'But, my dear,' Miss Francis smiled at her with surpassing sweetness. 'I think my mind must be going.' She lifted limp fingers from the keyboard and touched them to her forehead, as if to arrest the absconding mind. 'Hockey practices are on Tuesdays and Fridays. Choir practices are on Mondays and Thursdays. It was ever thus. Today is Thursday. Everyone else thinks it's Thursday, otherwise they

66

wouldn't be here.' She swept out a spare arm that encom-
passed the waiting choir, and asked helplessly, 'It *is* Thursday, isn't it? You all think it's Thursday? It's not just me
having a little brainstorm?'

The choir tittered, *sotto voce*, to assure Miss Francis that it
was indeed Thursday, and to express its mass contempt for
anyone who was fool enough to get caught in the cross-fire
between Miss Francis and Miss Taylor.

'It's a match against the High School, Miss Francis. Miss
Taylor called a special practice,' said Brenda, hoping that
her mention of the High School might save her, for if Miss
Francis loathed anyone more than she loathed Miss Taylor,
it was the music mistress at the High School. If the match
had been against the High School choir, it might have been a
different matter, and Miss Francis might have been out on
the side-lines chanting with the rest of them: 'Two – four –
six – eight, who – do – we – hate?'

Miss Francis, however, was not to be deflected. 'You
know that I do not allow any absence from choir without a
very good reason. Now, will you sit down, please?' She
turned gaily to face the room. 'I think we'll begin with the
Schubert.'

'Please. May I go and tell Miss Taylor that I can't come?'

Miss Francis sighed a sigh that turned a page on the music
stand.

'Two minutes, Brenda. We'll wait,' she said venomously,
and set the metronome ticking on the piano so that they
might all count the two minutes, second by second.

Miss Taylor still stood upon the steps of the Changing
Room. While they were all counting, they could turn round
and watch Brenda tell Miss Taylor that she was not allowed
to attend hockey practice.

Tock.

Tock.

Tock.

Brenda closed the door on the ticking and began to run.
She would have to run to be there and back in two minutes,
and running in the corridors was forbidden.

67

Miss Taylor had legs like bath loofahs stuffed into long, hairy grey socks, that were held up by tourniquets of narrow elastic. When she put on her stockings after school and mounted her bicycle to pedal strenuously home up East Hill, you could still see the twin red marks, like the rubber seals on Kilner jars. The loofahs were the first things that Brenda saw as she mounted the steps, and the grey socks bristled with impatience.

'Practice begins at twelve fifty,' said Miss Taylor. 'I suppose you were thinking of joining us?'

Brenda began to cringe all over again.

'Please, Miss Taylor, Miss Francis says I can't come.'

'Does she? And what's it got to do with Miss Francis? Are you in detention?'

'No, Miss Taylor. I'm in choir.'

'You may only be the goalkeeper, Brenda, but we still expect you to turn out for practices. You'll have to explain to Miss Francis that she must manage without you for once. I don't imagine that the choir will collapse if you're missing.'

'No, Miss Taylor.'

'Go on, then. At the double. We'll wait.'

Brenda ran down the steps, aware of the Music Room windows but not looking at them, and back into the corridor. Halfway along it she was halted by a shout from behind.

'*What* do you think you're doing?'

Brenda turned and saw the Head Girl, Gill Rogers, who was also the school hockey captain and had the sense not to try and sing as well.

'Running, Gill. Sorry, Gill.'

'Running's forbidden. You know that. Go back and walk.'

'Miss Taylor told me to run.'

'It's no good trying to blame Miss Taylor; I'm sure she didn't tell you to run.'

'She said at the double,' said Brenda.

'That's not the same thing at all. Go back and *walk*.'

Brenda went back and walked.

'Two minutes and fifteen seconds,' said Miss Francis, reaching for the metronome, when Brenda finally got back to

68

the Music Room. 'Sit down quickly, Brenda. Now then – I said sit down, Brenda.'

'Please, Miss Francis –'

A look of dire agony appeared on Miss Francis's face – it could have been wind so soon after lunch – and she held the metronome in a strangler's grip.

'I think you've delayed us long enough, Brenda.'

'Miss Taylor said couldn't you please excuse me from choir just this once as it's such an important match,' said Brenda, improvising rapidly, since Miss Taylor had said nothing of the sort. Miss Francis raised a claw.

'I believe I made myself perfectly clear the first time. Now, sit down, please.'

'But they're all waiting for me.'

'So are we, Brenda. I must remind you that it is not common practice in this school to postpone activities for the sake of Second Year girls. What position do you occupy in the team? First bat?' Miss Francis knew quite well that there are no bats required in a hockey game, but her ignorance suggested that she was above such things.

'Goalkeeper, Miss Francis.'

'Goalkeeper? From the fuss certain persons are making, I imagined that you must be at least a fast bowler. Is there no one else in the lower school to rival your undoubted excellence at keeping goal?'

'I *did* get chosen for the team, Miss Francis.'

'Clearly you have no equal, Brenda. That being the case, you hardly need to practise, do you?'

'Miss Taylor thinks I do,' said Brenda.

'Well, I'm afraid I don't. I would never, for one moment, keep you from a match, my dear, but a practice on a *Thursday* is an entirely different matter. Sit down.'

Brenda, panicking, pointed to the window. 'But she won't start without me.'

'Neither will I. You may return very quickly and tell Miss Taylor so. At once.'

Brenda set off along the corridor, expecting to hear the first notes of 'An die Musik' break out behind her. There was only silence. They were still waiting.

'Now run and get changed,' said Miss Taylor, swinging her whistle, as Brenda came up the steps again. 'We've waited long enough for you, my girl.'

'Miss Francis says I can't come,' Brenda said, baldly.

'Does she, now?'

'I've got to go back.' A scarcely suppressed jeer rose from the rest of the team, assembled in the Changing Room.

'Brenda, this is the Under-Thirteen Eleven, not the Under-Thirteen Ten. There must be at least sixty of you in that choir. Are you really telling me that your absence will be noticed?'

'Miss Francis'll notice it,' said Brenda.

'Then she'll just have to notice it,' said Miss Taylor under her breath, but loudly enough for Brenda to hear and appreciate. 'Go and tell Miss Francis that I insist you attend this practice.'

'Couldn't you give me a note, please?' said Brenda. Miss Taylor must know that any message sent via Brenda would be heavily edited before it reached its destination. She could be as insulting as she pleased in a note.

'A note?' Brenda might have suggested a dozen red roses thrown in with it. 'I don't see any reason to send a note. Simply tell Miss Francis that on this occasion she must let you go.'

Brenda knew that it was impossible to tell Miss Francis that she must do anything, and Miss Taylor knew it too. Brenda put in a final plea for mercy.

'Couldn't you tell her?'

'We've already wasted ten minutes, Brenda, while you make up your mind.'

'You needn't wait – '

'When I field a team, I field a team, not ten-elevenths of a team.' She turned and addressed the said team. 'It seems we'll have to stay here a little longer,' her eyes strayed to the Music Room windows, 'while Brenda arrives at her momentous decision.'

Brenda turned and went down the steps again.

'Hurry UP, girl.'

Miss Taylor's huge voice echoed dreadfully round the confining walls. She should have been in the choir herself, singing bass to Miss Humphry's tenor. Brenda began to run, and like a cuckoo from a clock, Gill Rogers sprang out of the cloakroom as she cantered past.

'Is that you again?'

Brenda side-stepped briskly and fled towards the Music Room, where she was met by the same ominous silence that had seen her off. The choir, cowed and bowed, crouched over the open music sheets and before them, wearing for some reason her *indomitable* expression, sat Miss Francis, tense as an overwound clockwork mouse and ready for action.

'At last. Really, Brenda, the suspense may prove too much for me. I thought you were never coming back.' She lifted her hands and brought them down sharply on the keys. The choir jerked to attention. An over-eager soprano chimed in and then subsided as Miss Francis raised her hands again and looked round. Brenda was still standing in the doorway.

'Please sit down, Brenda.'

Brenda clung to the door-post and looked hopelessly at Miss Francis. She would have gone down on her knees if there had been the slightest chance that Miss Francis would be moved.

'Well?'

'Please, Miss Francis, Miss Taylor says I *must* go to the practice. She wished devoutly that she were at home where, should rage break out on this scale, someone would have thrown something. If only Miss Francis would throw something; the metronome, perhaps, through the window.

Tock . . . tock . . . tock . . . *CRASH*! Tinkle tinkle.

But Miss Francis was a lady. With tight restraint she closed the lid of the piano.

'It seems,' she said, in a bitter little voice, 'that we are to have no music today. A hockey game is to take precedence over a choir practice.'

'It's *not* a game,' said Brenda. 'It's a practice, for a match. Just this once . . .?' she said, and was disgusted to find a tear

71

boiling up under her eyelid. 'Please, Miss Francis.'

'No, Brenda. I do not know why we are enduring this ridiculous debate (Neither do I, Miss Francis) but I thought I had made myself quite clear the first time you asked. You will not miss a scheduled choir practice for an unscheduled hockey practice. Did you not explain to Miss Taylor?'

'Yes I did!' Brenda cried. 'And she said you wouldn't miss me.'

Miss Francis turned all reasonable. 'Miss you? But my dear child, of course we wouldn't miss you. No one would miss you. You are not altogether indispensable, are you?'

'No, Miss Francis.'

'It's a matter of principle. I would not dream of abstracting a girl from a hockey team, or a netball team or even, heaven preserve us, from a shove-ha'penny team, and by the same token I will not allow other members of staff to disrupt my choir practices. Is that clear?'

'Yes, Miss Francis.'

'Go and tell Miss Taylor. I'm sure she'll see my point.'

'Yes, Miss Francis.' Brenda turned to leave, praying that the practice would at last begin without her, but the lid of the piano remained shut.

This time the Head Girl was waiting for her and had her head round the cloakroom door before Brenda was fairly on her way down the corridor.

'Why didn't you come back when I called you, just now?'

Brenda leaned against the wall and let the tear escape, followed by two or three others.

'Are you crying because you've broken rules,' Gill demanded, 'or because you got caught? I'll see you outside the Sixth-Form Room at four o'clock.'

'It's not my fault.'

'Of course it's your fault. No one forced you to run.'

'They're making me,' said Brenda, pointing two-handed in either direction, towards the Music Room and the Changing Room.

'I daresay you asked for it,' said Gill. 'Four o'clock, please,' and she went back into the Senior cloakroom in the

72

hope of catching some malefactor fiddling with the locks on the lavatory doors.

This last injustice gave Brenda a jolt that she might otherwise have missed, and the tears of self-pity turned hot with anger. She trudged along to the Changing Room.

'You don't exactly hurry yourself, do you?' said Miss Taylor. 'Well?'

'Miss Francis says I can't come to hockey, Miss Taylor.'

Miss Taylor looked round at the restive members of the Under-Thirteen XI and knew that for the good of the game it was time to make a stand.

'Very well, Brenda, I must leave it to you to make up your mind. Either you turn out now for the practice or you forfeit your place in the team. Which is it to be?'

Brenda looked at Miss Taylor, at the Music Room windows, and back to Miss Taylor.

'If I leave now, can I join again later?'

'Good Lord. Is there no end to this girl's cheek? Certainly not. This is your last chance, Brenda.'

It would have to be the choir. She could not bear to hear the singing and never again be part of it, Thursday after Monday, term after term. If you missed a choir practice without permission, you were ejected from the choir. There was no appeal. There would be no permission.

'I'll leave the team, Miss Taylor.'

She saw at once that Miss Taylor had not been expecting this. Her healthy face turned an alarming colour, like Lifebuoy kitchen soap.

'Then there's nothing more to say, is there? This will go on your report, you understand. I cannot be bothered with people who don't take things seriously.'

She turned her back on Brenda and blew the whistle at last, releasing the pent-up team from the Changing Room. They were followed, Brenda noticed, by Pat Stevens, the reserve, who had prudently put on the shin-pads in advance.

Brenda returned to the Music Room. The lid of the piano was still down and Miss Francis's brittle elbow pinned it.

'The prodigal returns,' she announced to the choir as

Brenda entered, having seen her approach down the corridor. 'It is now one fifteen. May we begin dear?'

'Yes, Miss Francis.'

'You finally persuaded Miss Taylor to see reason?'

'I told her what you said.'

'And?'

'She said I could choose between missing the choir practice and leaving the team.'

Miss Francis was transformed into an angular little effigy of triumph.

'I see you chose wisely, Brenda.'

'Miss Francis?'

'By coming back to the choir.'

'No, Miss Francis . . .' Brenda began to move towards the door, not trusting herself to come any closer to the piano. 'I'm going to miss choir practice. I came back to tell you.'

'Then you will leave the choir, Brenda. I hope you understand that.'

'Yes, Miss Francis.'

She stepped out of the room for the last time and closed the door. After a long while she heard the first notes of the piano, and the choir finally began to sing. Above the muted voices a whistle shrilled, out on the playing-field. Brenda went and sat in the Junior cloakroom, which was forbidden in lunch hour, and cried. There was no rule against that.

The Toad

Melanie Bush

The day I finished Kafka's *Metamorphosis* Father disappeared and a toad appeared in the cellar. At first the connection between Kafka's story and Father's disappearance did not occur to me. How could Father turn into a toad? Yet as the days went by and there was still no sign of Father I began to wonder. Was the slimy toad which sat faintly pulsating in the cellar under the work table my father? Impossible! And yet . . .

I spent most of the evening watching the toad, trying to find some resemblance between Dad and this creature. It was proving hard. The fat toad did nothing but sit there, staring at me with its glassy, eyelid-twitching eyes. It occasionally made an odd sort of belching noise. Surely this could not be Dad. The toad was an ugly brown colour with huge eyes which stuck out of its head. Every so often, when some unwary spider scuttled by, the toad's tongue would flick out. Seconds later the spider was nothing but a tasty morsel. The toad was deadly accurate. It never missed. I think it was this accuracy which convinced me of the toad's identity. It reminded me that my father was the best bowler in the Brayington cricket club first team. I realised that, although his outward appearance had changed considerably, this damp creature was my father.

Now I knew that the toad was Father my opinion of it altered. It was no longer 'the toad' but became 'my toad'. It was not quite so fat and ugly. Father could not possibly be allowed to live in the dark, dank cellar. I went upstairs and into the kitchen.

'Mum?' I asked.

'Yes?'

'Well, er, well. You may not believe this but there's a toad in the cellar.'

'That's not unusual,' she interrupted.

'But this one is Dad!'

She threw back her head and laughed. Put that way, I suppose it did sound a bit stupid.

'It's true,' I said.

She continued to laugh. I was about to lose my temper.

'I don't see how you can laugh when your husband is sitting in that cellar gulping down spiders,' I hissed at her.

She only laughed.

'Don't you care?' I screamed at her.

She was angry now.

'Don't you speak to me like that either,' she shouted back.

'And don't you shout at me!'

She started to laugh again. She refused to take me seriously.

'I have just read Kafka's *Metamorphosis* in which a man woke up and found he was a beetle. My father has just disappeared and a large toad has turned up in the cellar. I have put two and two together . . .'

'And got five,' interrupted my brother who entered the room at that moment. 'What's the matter with her?' He jerked his thumb at Mum.

'She finds something very amusing,' said I sarcastically.

'She says your father has changed into a toad,' Mum burst out.

This set my brother off as well. I watched them both and thought how stupid they were. I walked out of the room. I returned to the cellar. The toad was still sitting under the work table. I fetched a cardboard box from my bedroom. There was still one problem. Even though the toad was my father I still could not bring myself to touch it. In the end I had to resort to the coal shovel. I took the box upstairs and placed it in front of the coal fire in the sitting room. The toad remained in the box for several minutes. It then struggled out, using all the strength it possessed. With a disturbing hop it was seated on the best arm-chair. This toad, without a doubt, was Father. I left the room.

'Sarah?' came a small voice from the top of the stairs.

'Yes?' It was my younger brother, John.

'When is Daddy coming home?'

'He is home except . . . well, he's changed quite a lot,' I answered.

John just looked at me.

'Where is he?' he asked innocently.

'In the sitting room . . .'

I was speaking to the wall. John had gone. I only wished that I could have explained first. I followed him into the sitting room. The small figure stood in the middle of the room gazing around.

'He's not there. You lied,' came a reproachful murmur.

I did not know quite what to say.

'And what's that nasty old toad doing on Dad's chair?'

In the corner stood a wing-back arm-chair upholstered in red velvet. In the centre of the plump cushion sat the toad. The ugly toad was staring at us. He was ugly! I could not be persuaded to think otherwise.

'That toad is Dad,' I replied.

My brother looked at me and then laughed in delight. He loved to be teased.

'You're teasing,' he said.

'No, that's the truth.'

He walked over to the toad and began to talk to it, addressing it as 'Dad'.

'No, really and truly. Where's Dad?' he persisted.

'Dad has changed to be a toad.'

'Like a princess?'

'No, not like a princess.'

'How do you know?'

He was right. How did I know? It had seemed obvious before, but now I was not so sure.

'I read a book where a man turned into a beetle.'

'Oh! Then it must be Dad.'

The little figure crouched by the velvet chair and said:

'Today we made pictures of Father Christmas and mine was the best.'

No answer.

'We wrote stories and mine is to be put upon the wall.'

No answer.

'Are you listening, Daddy?'

The toad belched.

'How I wish I could speak toad language,' the boy declared dolefully. 'It's going to be hard to have our little talks now.'

I left them to it.

Our house is the type with inch-thick walls separating each room. As you enter the house by the front door there is a sitting room on your right and a little further on is the kitchen. From the kitchen came the laughter of my Mum and brother. They could not understand. Then I could hear Mum talking. She seemed concerned. Her voice was low so I could only catch some of the words. She was talking about my father. I did not want to listen. My father was a toad and that was that.

'Does Mum know about Dad?' came my little brother's voice.

'Yeah, but she doesn't believe me.'

'She doesn't?' His face expressed amazement. 'I'm going to tell her.'

'Go on, then. She'll just laugh.'

He ran through to the kitchen. I could hear his plaintive voice explaining the situation to Mum. She was not laughing.

'Who told you that?' she asked.

'Sarah.'

'Do you believe her?'

'Yes. She read a book.'

'Sarah, Sarah. Come here immediately,' Mum shouted. I went to the kitchen.

'Yes.'

'What rubbish have you been telling your brother?'

'The same as I told you,' I answered.

Nobody spoke. Mum was shaking and then she was crying. At first she tried to hide the tears but soon she was sobbing uncontrollably. She stood up and left the room. She paused at the door. She looked rundown.

'And you, stop making up stories about your father. It's bad enough without you . . .'

She was unable to finish. She broke down in tears. She took one look at the room before running upstairs. The three of us just stared at each other.

'What's the matter with her?'

'I don't know,' replied my elder brother.

I thought he did know. He looked apprehensive. His hands shook slightly.

'What's for dinner?' said my younger brother. He was not old enough to realise that Mum was in a state.

'I dunno.'

He accepted that.

'Sarah, you'd better shut up about Father, you know. Mum is pretty cut up about it,' said my elder brother.

'What, about her husband being a toad?'

'Look, Dad has gone and I reckon she thinks he has gone for good. She wanted to put off telling you. It doesn't help: you making up stories.'

'I'm not making up stories.'

'It's all true,' chipped in John.

'Look, just stop it. It's only upsetting her.'

'The story, as you call it, about Dad being the toad is true,' I asserted.

My brother opened his mouth to speak.

'It's not a story, it's not made up,' I screamed at him.

'Sorry I spoke,' he replied.

From then on there was a definite split in the family. John and I seemed to be the optimists and my elder brother and mother were the realists. It made life difficult. At about eight o'clock Mum reappeared and set about preparing tea. She made a lot of noise in the process. She refused to say a word and simply gave us filthy looks. Her face was blotchy from crying. John and I went through to the sitting room and played Monopoly. It was a good game. The toad looked on.

'Your tea is ready,' said Mum, poking her head round the door.

We trooped through to the kitchen. Mum slammed a plate of spaghetti in front of each of us. She sat down and stared at her plate. My younger brother slurped away at his spaghetti. My older brother did not eat in his normal, hearty manner. I ate but felt self-conscious. Every scrape or clatter of cutlery on plate seemed to cut through me.

'Mum, I'm sorry if I upset you, but it is true.'

'I am not interested,' she answered with a forced smile.

'You should read the book.'

'Be quiet.'

She began to pick at her food.

'The toad . . .'

'Shut up about the toad,' she shouted at me.

'O.K. I will.'

I picked up my plate and left the room. John followed me out, slamming the door behind him. In silence, we finished our meal in the sitting room.

'And don't forget to bring your plates back after you,' she screamed.

We did not answer her. The toad still sat in the pride of place. My elder brother opened the door.

'Sarah?'

'What?'

'The book, can I borrow it?'

'Sure.'

One thing that had not occurred to me in bringing the toad upstairs from the cellar was what to feed it on. Flies were the obvious answer. There were a couple buzzing around the bay window. The newspaper was at hand and after several attempts I managed to kill both of them. Toad demolished them in seconds. Maybe we should have left it in the cellar. Yes! I could put him back. But he was my father. It was an impossible situation. I either had to look after and feed a large toad which was not an easy task or I would have to turn my father out of the house. I had to look after the toad, even though it would upset my mother.

We sat and watched TV for a while. My elder brother was sprawled across the couch reading *Metamorphosis*. John was constructing a Lego model.

'Sarah, I think you've got it,' my elder brother exclaimed.

'Got what?' I replied suspiciously.

'That toad. It could be Dad.'

'Oh, then it's not such a stupid idea now, is it? Now you agree it must be a toad,' I replied.

He looked surprised.

'Sorry, there's not need to be sarcastic,' he said.

I just shrugged my shoulders. He was only baiting me. I snuggled into the chair and tried to sulk. He did not say anything. He continued reading; I continued to sulk.

'Sarah, I believe you. I'm not just being sarky,' he said.

'Honestly?'

He just nodded. At that moment a comedy duo came onto the screen. It really was funny and set us all laughing. My brother continued to read the book. He seemed to find it interesting.

'It's time for bed,' called Mum.

We all trooped upstairs to bed. I now realised that instead of a two/two split it was now a three to one split. We were succeeding, but it was upsetting Mum. I lay awake for hours worrying about our toad.

The following day was Saturday. We got up at the normal time but Mum lay in bed most of the morning. The toad was still seated in the chair. It seemed dopey and its skin was rather dry. I placed some bread and milk before it, but it hardly ate any. However, then my elder brother brought a dish of dead flies. The toad gobbled them up eagerly.

'Hello. Is this the famous toad?' said Mum in a pleasant voice. Normally I would have asked her why she had got up late, implying that she was lazy, but today I could not bring myself to do it. I frowned. Why had she suddenly changed? I knew her moods well. She usually took time to get over them. Could my toad, the one she called famous, be the same toad that she was having a fit about only last night?

'What are you frowning for, Sarah?'

'Nothing, Mum.'

'I've been reading that book of yours. Maybe I misjudged you. Your idea about Dad is good.'

'You really think so?'

'Yes,' she said. 'And I suppose he is hungry.'

'You bet he is.'

She walked over and patted the toad on the head.

'He has changed a lot.'

The three of us could not believe our eyes. It was amazing. She went through to the kitchen to prepare some toad food. The toad seemed contented. It began to move about. It hopped off the chair and made its way across the carpet which was the same muddy colour as itself. Mum entered.

'Mum!' I screamed.

It was too late. Mum had trodden it into the carpet. My younger brother began to whimper. Mum's face filled with horror and grief. Then the door bell rang and we heard someone entering by the front door. The day Mum trod on the toad was the day Dad returned home.

The Aggie Match

Lynne Reid Banks

Ronnie was a lonely little boy. He lived with his father and mother on a farm in Canada. He had no brothers or sisters, and no friends either, because the farm was far away from everywhere.

When he looked out of his bedroom window, or any other window of the wooden farm house, all he could see was miles and miles and miles of flat wheat-fields. Sometimes they were covered with green or golden wheat, which rippled in the wind like the waves of the sea. In autumn there was only stubble, which made Ronnie feel sad because it looked so dead and finished. In the winter deep snow fell, and then Ronnie's window-world was white, white, white, and flat as far as he could see.

A long straight road ran past Ronnie's house. It came from far away in one direction, got wider and wider till it came to the farm; then it started to get narrower again as it stretched away towards the far-off horizon. There it came to a point and disappeared. It was a very dull road, with never a bend in it, and nothing on either side but the wheat-fields, and telegraph poles. But Ronnie always began each day by running to the window of his bedroom and looking along it one way, then running out, across the corridor at the top of the wooden stairs and into his mother's and father's room, to look along it the other way.

And sometimes – not very often – he would see a car or a truck somewhere along those empty miles of road. He would hang out of the window, watching the moving speck get nearer and nearer; when it passed one special telegraph pole he knew he must rush down the stairs and out of doors to be by the roadside when it went roaring past. And afterwards he ran up the stairs again to hang out of the window on the other side of the house and watch the car or truck become a tiny speck again. He liked these times very much, but he always felt depressed after them.

Ronnie was nearly eight. For a long time now, his mother had been talking about him going to school. Ronnie wanted to go to school more than he wanted anything in the world, more than a bicycle or even a pony. At school would be other children. At school there would be lots of noise.

Ronnie didn't hate living on the farm; it was all he knew. But he hated the quiet. He used to stand outdoors and listen for sounds. There was the singing of birds, and the sound of his father's tractor sometimes, or, if he stood by the kitchen window, the sounds his mother made, filling the stove with cut wood or bumping the legs of the table with the broom or clicking the wooden spoon against the sides of the bowl when she was making cake. They were all nice sounds, but there were not nearly enough of them.

The sound of people's voices was what Ronnie wanted most.

His father and mother were very nearly the only people Ronnie ever saw, or heard. And they were both very quiet. When his father came in at night after work, he was tired. He didn't talk much. His mother talked sometimes, but she, too, was always very busy. Sometimes when Ronnie wanted to talk he would go into the kitchen and stand by the door and stare at her and hope she would speak to him. Sometimes she noticed him and said something, but it was usually something like 'Is anything wrong? Why don't you play outside?' Then she would probably give him a cookie and shoo him out again because he was in her way.

Often he said to her, 'When will I go to school, Mother?' And she'd say, 'When we find a way to take you.'

Ronnie understood this problem. The school was in Town, and Town was a hundred miles away. How could a person's father, who anyway had to get up at dawn to do his work, find time to drive a person a hundred miles to school?

Going into Town in the farm truck was something they did once a month. It was the greatest thing in Ronnie's life. He counted the days, starting with the day after a visit, and because of this he could count backwards from thirty before he could count forwards.

'How many days left now, Mother?'

'Twenty-nine – twenty-eight – twenty-seven – twenty-six . . .' all the way down to 'One more. Tomorrow we're going.'

On one-more nights, Ronnie couldn't sleep, at least not till late, going to Town was so exciting. There was the general store, where his mother handed in a long list of supplies and the man piled the huge bags of flour and sugar and potatoes and the tins of jam and the big dried-up-looking chunks of meat into an enormous box which his father put into the back of the truck. And there was the street full of people and cars and bicycles and trucks, and sometimes horses. And the railway station with its trains and the big grain-elevators standing up against the sky.

And the people! Lots and lots of them, all talking and laughing and shouting and making lovely, peopley noises. There were children too, though Ronnie was too shy to speak to any of them. He just liked to stand near his mother as she shopped, or hang around outside and watch them running and playing.

They seemed to know how to play in a way that he didn't. For one thing, they had toys. Ronnie had very few toys. He had an old skipping-rope that he couldn't skip with, although he knew a lot of other things to do with it; and a cardboard boat that his mother had made him from one of the store-boxes, with two sticks for oars; and a football, though that had burst and wasn't much good; and an old hobby-horse that his father had made him long ago. He also had a lot of bits and pieces that nobody else wanted, like a worn-out tractor tyre, and some broken dishes, and a bent spoon for digging and an old hammer for hammering nails, and some empty paint-tins, and a length of chain, and some other things like that.

But his favourite toy was a glass marble. He'd found it one

day in the street of the Town, and his mother had said he could keep it.

As soon as the first real mud of the big thaw had begun to dry, leaving patches of dark bare earth, the boys of the Town and some girls too would crouch round a little hole they made with a stick. They took their marbles ('aggies' they called them) out of little bags, and tried to knock them into the hole with crooked forefingers. There were many rules and words connected with the game, which Ronnie, watching from a safe distance, was beginning to master.

He knew that you could, if you were clever, win aggies from other children – that some children went home with bulging bags and others, sadly, with flat empty ones. He had seen one little boy cry because he had lost all his aggies. But then he had run to his mother, who was in the store with Ronnie's own mother, buying things, and she had at once bought him a whole new bag of aggies and he had joined in the game again.

Such incidents puzzled Ronnie. Why had some people a lot of money and others, like his family, so little? Why did some people live in Town and go to school and have friends, or even brothers and sisters, and people like himself live far away out on the prairie? Why, come to that, did some children have chatty, gossiping, laughing mothers, and hearty fathers who slapped each other on the back and got red faces and louder voices in the town Bar, when his mother and father were so silent and serious?

But one question worried Ronnie more than these. Other children could talk and laugh together, run up to each other and say, 'Let's play!' One boy could give another boy a push so they rolled over together, fighting and struggling, and then they were friends afterwards. How could they open their mouths and shout and yell, and throw their bodies about without worrying about getting hurt or dirty? Why did they seem so free, when he felt so shut-in?

He would stand in the street, always close to a building or a car so that he didn't feel too exposed, and preferably in the shadows, and watch them, and wish he were like them. Even when their mothers called them and they were rude, or took no notice, or ran away to play round a corner – even when a mother or father, infuriated, would give chase and drag a child back, scolding or shaking him, shouting at him for getting his clothes muddy or being disobedient – even then, Ronnie envied them. When his own mother or father called, he always ran at once – he meant not to, he meant to be naughty like the others, but his body obeyed before he had time to tell it not to. He was used to obeying.

One Town-day he was standing silently watching an aggie-match. It was taking place in a patch of spring sunshine beside the wooden store-building. There was a vacant lot there, with bushes and tall grasses, where Ronnie had watched the children playing hide-and-seek and other more complicated games, but near the building was a patch of earth on a little rise which always dried out early. This was always the first aggie-ground to come into use each year, and there was usually a fight for first rights to it.

The game was getting very exciting. Only three boys were left with any marbles. Two of them had won away from the others all they had. Now the third of the boys had only two aggies left, and they were both his beauties; he said he never played with them because he didn't want to risk losing them.

Ronnie was close enough to see them, in fact he was quite familiar with them because he had seen this boy take them out of his pocket and look at them lovingly. One was a large, dark blue one with something like a flower inside. But the other was the best. It was a pale yellow, no, not quite yellow, sort of gold – Ronnie could not think of anything he knew which was exactly the same colour, except perhaps the wheat when it first lost its green, before it turned that hard straw-yellow. It was plain glass except for a scattering of tiny, tiny bubbles inside, and it was perfect, no scratches or chips like the 'working' aggies soon got when they were much played with. Ronnie saw the boy who owned this treasure holding it up to the light and gazing at it with the same wonder as he felt

87

himself. The other two boys waited, pretending scorn but actually with the light of greed in their eyes.

'Aw, g'wan – play it! What use is an aggie if you never play it?'

'Only girls keep the pretty ones and don't chance 'em!'

'It'll get scratched,' said the third boy.

'Maybe you'll get it straight in. Maybe it'll be a lucky one for you, and you'll win our two and won't have to play your goldie any more.'

'Anyways, if you don't play it, you're out of the game.'

The boy made his decision.

'I'll play my bluey first. But you two gotta play your beauties too.'

'Okay!'

The group of players who had fallen out crowded round to watch. Their grime-backed forefingers, with which they had been shooting the aggies, twitched in sympathy as the boy spat on his bluey and rubbed it on his sleeve for luck. The three players stood with toes on a scratched line, and at the signal they threw their aggies towards the hole.

Ronnie moved nearer. He had to, or he couldn't see. He crouched behind the line of other children, and peered through their legs. The three aggies rolled, and settled. The bluey came to rest within eighteen inches of the hole; it was the nearest. That meant the owner of the bluey would play first.

He crouched beside the furthest-away marble, a light green one with a red spiral in it called a twisty. If he could shoot this one into the hole, he could try for the next-furthest, and then finally the nearest, his own. But the other two boys had been cunning. They had deliberately let him get his bluey the nearest, and thrown theirs short. He hadn't a hope of getting the twisty in; he shot hard – it left the ground and leapt past the hole. He straightened up with a grim face.

The second boy shot his own marble. It was a 'bird's-egg', a china marble with gold speckles on it. Ronnie envied this one the least, since what use was a marble if you couldn't see the light through it? But the gold flecks made it special. The boy took a long time over his shot, measuring the distance with his eyes, and swinging his bent finger back and forth like a golf-club. Ronnie held his breath. He wanted the bluey-boy to win. The others had so many, and the bluey-boy only the two beauties.

The shot came at last, and Ronnie was sure it was going in – it rolled along the uneven ground, bumping over the small half-submerged pebbles, its gold flakes glittering bravely – right to the brink of the hole. But it was a tricky hole. It had a rim, almost invisible but still enough to stop an aggie whose force was nearly spent. The bird's-egg was halted by it, just when it was about to drop in. The shooter let out a groan and Ronnie gave a sigh of relief.

The third boy stepped forward with a careless swagger. The twisty (now about a foot on the far side of the hole) was his best marble; he was playing it only to show off, and because he felt confident that he could win both the bird's-egg and the bluey, for he had plenty of other beauties he could have used. His strategy had worked so far; he had aimed to shoot last, reckoning that the other two, less experienced players, would both muff their shots and leave the field in good order for him to scoop all three aggies. So it seemed it would be, for his twisty was less than a foot on the far side of the hole where it had been overshot by the bluey-boy: the bird's-egg quivered on the very brink, where the most careless flick would tip it home; and the coveted bluey itself was still where it had first fallen, by no means too far for an expert like him to shoot it in. After he had done this, it would be child's play to win the others.

There was only one problem, and even Ronnie, with his incomplete knowledge of the game, could see what it was. The bird's-egg was in a direct line with the bluey that had to be shot first. They were playing according to the rule which says that if you touch one aggie with another, the next player collects any aggies you get into the hole. This meant that if the expert hit the bird's-egg in with the bluey, and if the bluey itself went in after it, then the bluey's owner would get them both, and the next turn as well.

There was only one way out. The expert had to shoot the bluey in a curve, avoiding the bird's-egg. This is possibly the most difficult shot there is, because even the breath of a passing aggie might shiver the bird's-egg in, and then who was to say whether they had actually touched or not? The expert hesitated, and then tried tactics.

'Knockers keepers,' he said as he crouched down.

He said it in a very casual tone, as if merely confirming what everybody knew. But there was an instant outcry from the other players, and from the crowd who had been playing earlier.

'Nuts to that! We haven't been playing knockers keepers all day!'

'Well, we are now.'

'We are not!'

'We are so. Every game is separate. Nobody called knockers losers for this game.'

'You don't have to call for each game! If nobody calls something different, it's same as the last game.'

'Well, I just did call something different.'

But he was howled down. He gave in fairly gracefully, having hardly expected to get away with his ploy. He shrugged his shoulders.

'Okay, okay. I don't care. I can still do it.'

A deep hush fell, and Ronnie, hardly aware of what he was doing, edged into the front line with the others to see better. The third player crouched down, his gangling knees up to his ears. His dirt-grained finger crooked behind the bluey. Ronnie saw its owner clutch the sides of his jacket in an agony of suspense.

The bluey moved off in a slow, deliberate curve. It was a beautiful shot, and it had to be. There wasn't a sound from the crowd as it rolled, as if under its own power, round in a wide arc, missing the poised bird's-egg and dropping nearly into the little earth cavity.

It lay there like a blue eye looking out of the ground.

A sound half-way between a sigh and a moan went round

the circle. Ronnie couldn't look at the other boy. He stared at that unwinking lost eye.

Its new owner leapt up gleefully and pocketed it. He was so pleased with himself that he didn't even crouch for the next shot, but simply bent over from the waist and flicked the twisty towards the hole with a limp swing of his arm from the elbow. The chatter which had started among the children in response to his previous clever shot died on the instant; the twisty spun unerringly across the intervening space, in down one side of the hole, up the other, and then fell back into place – bringing the bird's-egg on top of it with a little final click.

Nobody spoke. Now Ronnie could look at the other boy. His hands were slowly relaxing on the edge of his jacket. He glanced uncertainly from face to face, not quite able to believe his luck. The third boy gave him a not unfriendly push from behind, and he stumbled forward and clumsily picked up the two aggies nestling together in the hole.

'I guess that's one way to win,' said the loser disgustedly.

'Sore loser!' taunted the crowd.

'Okay! Now you got three beauties. So play me again. Play your goldie!'

'No!'

'No fair to quit when you're winning.'

The bluey-boy scuffed his sneakers on the hard ground. He made a decision.

'Okay then. I'll play my goldie if you'll play my bluey!'

The richer boy tossed the bluey into the air and caught it again several times. It glittered like a precious sapphire in the thin sunlight.

'Want it back, huh? Think you can beat me? You only got those two through my bad luck.'

'You want to play, or don't you?'

'Sure!'

'Twosies!' suddenly said the other boy, the one who had lost the bird's-egg.

Ronnie was so caught up in the game by now that he forgot his shyness.

91

'What's "twosies"?' he asked the boy standing next to him.

'Don't you know? It means everyone throws two aggies.'

Though he had never been to school or been taught arithmetic, Ronnie saw at once that this meant twice as many aggies – six instead of three – and twice as much excitement. He could not help jumping up and down once, but he quickly took hold of himself.

The three players were once more poised on the throwing-line. Ronnie saw that his favourite player was having trouble deciding which aggie to hold on to, which two to play. Eventually he settled on the goldie and the twisty, retaining the bird's-egg.

The other two were not obliged to risk two beauties each, so they played one beauty and one ordinary aggie. The bird's-egg boy, smarting from its loss, carefully selected his least treasured beauty, a fairly common cat's-eye in good condition, which, Ronnie thought, only just counted as a beauty at all.

The signal was given, and the six aggies flashed, landed, rolled. The ground seemed covered with them. Ronnie gripped his hand hard round his own precious solitary aggie, like a talisman. As the bluey-boy moved to take the first shot, he caught Ronnie's eye. Ronnie swallowed. He gave a little nod of his head, a stiff little movement, with which he wanted to convey encouragement and support. The bluey-boy's face lost its grim look for a moment and he almost smiled.

The game moved quickly. The rich boy, as Ronnie thought of him, the riches being measured in aggies though he was the poorest-dressed, collared three aggies with his first turn, but two of them were the ordinary ones and the third the twisty which had been his to begin with. Still on the ground were the cat's-eye, the bluey – and the goldie, upon which every eye was hungrily fixed. They were all grouped near the hole, and it seemed certain that the other boy, whose turn it was, would get them all in one by one.

Ronnie was so keyed up he felt he couldn't bear to watch

the ground. The aggies seemed to be dancing, he had concentrated on them for so long. So he decided to watch the bluey-boy's face instead, and guess from that what was happening.

It was not difficult, for a grim face can always grow three degrees grimmer, and that is what happened. His mouth tightened, drew down at the corners – one aggie gone. Ronnie was dying to see which, but even though he cheated with himself and glanced down, all he could see was the player's back as he scrabbled like a crab into position for the next shot. The face he was watching changed again to an expression of agonized expectation, teeth bared, brows frowning. Was this the goldie? The shot was taken in perfect silence; there was a gasp – then a sigh, and every head turned to look at the boy who was now immeasurably poorer than he had been a moment before.

Ronnie didn't have to look down to know that the goldie had passed to a new possessor. He lowered his eyes to his own sneakers. He knew the loser of this treasure must cry, who could help it? – and he didn't want to watch that.

The final aggie, not that it mattered now, followed the goldie into the already bulging bag of the bird's-egg boy.

The crowd began to break up.

'You want to play your last aggie?'

With lowered face, the boy shook his head. He was desperate enough however to try something. Ronnie saw him approach the third boy.

'Trade you.'

'What?'

'Your bird's-egg for my goldie.'

'You're nuts.'

Everyone had moved away now. The two winners were crouching together, gloating over their spoils; their aggies, tipped out of the bags, lay in carefully separated piles. Ronnie still stood there, fascinated, unable to move away from the scene of the battle, the sight of so much wealth.

Suddenly one of them noticed him.

'Say, kid,' he said, 'you got any aggies?'

93

'One.'

'You wanna play?'

Ronnie shook his head.

'Let's see what kind you got.'

Ronnie hesitated. Burnt into his memory was an incident he had once witnessed. A boy, smaller and even more timid than himself, had been persuaded into showing some bigger boys a toy from his pocket. A swift blow on the wrist had knocked the toy to the ground, whence it had been snatched up and made off with, its rightful owner left in the middle of the street howling with helpless outrage.

He looked from one boy to the other.

'You gonna grab it off me if I show you?'

'Naw! Why should we? We only wanna look. Is it a beauty?'

Slowly Ronnie drew his hand from his pocket, and held it before him. He uncurled the protective fingers a little, to show the aggie nestling in his palm. Its smooth, unplayed surface was misted with the heat of his hand, but the boys could see it was a rare treasure indeed – smaller than the usual size, and of a beautiful, glowing red.

'A peewee ruby!' breathed one. 'Boy!'

'It's a beauty all right!' agreed the other. 'Where'd you get it?'

'Found it,' said Ronnie, returning it to his pocket.

'Let's see it again.'

This time Ronnie dared to open his hand all the way. The peewee ruby glowed in his palm like fire and blood.

'Trade you.'

'What for?'

The boy moved to his pile and quickly selected his three best marbles, including the new-won goldie, and pocketed them.

'Any one of these others.'

'Naw.'

'Okay then. Any two.'

Ronnie felt a surge of delight pass over him. It was his first taste of power. At his feet lay riches, and the pleasures of free choice. But he looked again at his own aggie. No. It had been precious enough before, but since he had learnt its name and that it was coveted, its value had trebled.

'Naw.'

The boy debated with himself. 'Tell you what then. I'll lend you one to play with. If you win, you can keep it and I'll give you two others, any two you choose except my three beauties. If I win, you gotta give me your peewee.'

Ronnie was on the point of shaking his head again when he saw the other boy – the one who had lost all, or nearly all, his aggies – standing at some distance, watching them.

'I can't play. I never played.'

The two big boys looked at each other in comic astonishment.

'Where've ya bin? Ya musta bin drug up in a barn!'

Ronnie, who was unfamiliar with this taunt said nothing. To him a barn held no insulting connotations, it was a fact of the landscape.

The bird's-egg boy spoke up again. His greed for the peewee ruby would not allow him to let Ronnie go.

'Okay, listen. I'll go easy on you. Tell you what. I'll play with my left hand. Waddaya say? Ain't that fair?'

Ronnie, who didn't know his left from his right, stood stock still, looking at the other boy in confusion.

'Okay?' he pressed.

'I dunno.'

'Aw, c'mon,' said the third boy. 'He don't wanna. Let him alone.'

The bird's-egg boy ignored him. 'What *would* you play for?' he persisted.

Ronnie muttered something.

'Whatcha say?'

'The goldie.'

'The *goldie*? Aw, heck . . .'

The third boy nudged him hard. 'Go ahead. You can't lose, can you? He's just a baby. He ain't never even played.' He had scented an exciting contest.

'Okay. Your peewee against my goldie!'

Ronnie's throat closed up with horror and his heart threatened to thud out of his chest and away down the road by itself. He put a hand up to his breastbone as if to hold it in, and his peewee fell and rolled on the ground. Instantly he snatched it up. He wanted to cry. He thought he was going to. What had he done? The aggie he loved was as good as lost.

The crowd of children had magically reassembled, as if, scattered about the street and vacant lot, they had sensed the onset of a new match. The bluey-boy stood aside, as Ronnie had at first.

Now it was Ronnie's grubby sneaker-toe on the line, newly defined in the grit with a sharp stick. Standing side by side with his opponent, he felt his essential inferiority to this tough, worldly-wise, practised towny boy. Older than Ronnie, two inches taller, his hair untouched by a brush, his legs filthy, he was everything Ronnie was not and longed to be. And soon he would own Ronnie's aggie, and thus would have everything in the world that mattered.

'Okay, let's call the rules,' he said competently. 'Ya wanna call something?'

Ronnie looked at him mutely.

'Knockers takers or knockers losers?'

'I dunno.'

'Knockers takers,' he said. 'Ya want inners winners?'

'What is it?'

The older boy rolled his eyes up for the benefit of the audience.

'You don't know nothin', do ya? It's if you get your aggie straight in with your first throw, you collect both aggies and the game's over.'

Ronnie looked at the hole. It was so far away – impossible to dream he could throw it in or anywhere near in.

'G'wan,' urged his opponent craftily. 'The peewee's smaller, it'll roll in easier.' The opposite was in fact the truth, as he knew. Smaller, lighter aggies were the hardest to win with. When he himself had got possession of the peewee he would keep it as a trophy, never play it. Among sophisticated players, peewees were never played against regular aggies,

96

only in special peewee matches.

'Okay then,' said Ronnie hopelessly. What difference could it make?

'On your mark. Get set. Throw!'

Ronnie didn't even know how to do that properly. He instinctively felt that the regulation underarm throw would not bring the aggie anywhere near the mark. So he raised his arm over his shoulder and tossed the ruby, with a feeling of angry desperation, in the general direction of the hole.

The crowd broke into laughter as the peewee performed a series of bounces, overtaking the goldie which was rolling decorously down the straight in the approved fashion.

Ronnie hated the laughter. He watched the peewee bouncing and knew it must be getting scratched; he felt each impact on his own flesh. He had thrown his treasure away, and for what? Because another boy had looked sad? Because he wanted the goldie for himself? He couldn't understand. A moment ago the ruby had been part of his pocket, part of his hand, part of his existence. Now it had disappeared somewhere down there in a blur of tears and he would never touch it again.

But something was wrong. The laughter had stopped on a sudden jarring note, and everyone was bent forward, peering.

'Geez!' came an awe-stricken whisper. 'It's in!'

'The kid got it right in!'

'It's inners winners – he's won 'em both, first throw!'

Ronnie brushed his tears away with a hand still innocent of contact with the gritty ground. He looked incredulously at the hole. His little red aggie winked at him from smack in the middle of it. The goldie lay a good foot away, catching the sun like a solid gold pearl.

Someone gave him a shove.

'Go get 'em, kiddo. They're yours!'

The other boy was justifiably dumbfounded and furious.

'No fair – ' he began, but was drowned out by hoots and jeers. The crowd, who had recently tasted the bitterness of defeat and beggary at the hands of this marble-millionaire,

97

was delighted at the chance to turn on him in his discomfiture.

'Shut up, sore loser! It was *you* called inners winners!'

'He'd a beat you anyhow! He's a genius!'

Several hands banged Ronnie on the back as he walked unsteadily to the hole. He bent down. As his hands touched, simultaneously, the peewee and the goldie, as he lifted them and held them side by side to the light, he felt a queer sensation. It was, in actual fact, his first experience of tangible, definite, positive happiness. It was so strong it was possible to confuse it with pain, and he felt he might cry again.

The boy he had been playing with was muttering something about beginners' luck, but Ronnie didn't hear. He started to walk away, oblivious of everything except that he held a beautiful aggie in each hand. Something gripped his arm.

'Ya wanna play again? Twosies?'

Ronnie shook free. 'Naw!' he said.

'Aw, c'mon! No fair to quit when you're –'

But Ronnie was already running, running back round the corner of the store where his father's truck was parked. He scrambled inside the cabin which felt like a haven. He could not but suppose they would come after him like a pack of hounds to drag him back and force him to yield up his miraculously won prizes. But safely in the cabin, high off the ground and surrounded by solid steel and glass, he felt secure.

He laid a hand on each knee, opened the fingers slowly, and gazed. Relief and happiness poured over him, he sank into it and it engulfed him as solidly as a billion grains of wheat when you jump into a heap of them, and work yourself down till you are buried to the neck.

Suddenly someone tapped on the glass by his head. He started with fright and thrust the aggies back into his pockets.

It was the bluey-boy. He had climbed up on the outside of the truck and was hanging on by the door-handle, his face level with Ronnie's.

Ronnie rolled down the window.

'Whatcha want?'

The boy looked at him dumbly for a moment.

'Willya trade?' he croaked at last.

'What for?'

'My – the goldie for the bird's-egg.'

'Naw!' cried Ronnie instantly, adding, like the bigger boys, 'Are you nuts?'

The other boy's lips trembled.

'I had it years already,' he said. 'It was always my best beauty.'

'So whyja play it then?'

'Whyja play yours?'

Ronnie was silenced. He did not understand to this moment what had possessed him to risk losing his aggie.

'Something gets hold of ya,' muttered the other boy.

Neither of them spoke for a while. The boy changed hands and hung on to the handle precariously.

'What's your name?' asked Ronnie.

'Gordie,' said the other. He gave his nose a quick wipe on his sleeve, bending his head down to his arm to do it. 'You won't trade me, then?'

'I dunno.'

'What's yours?'

'Ronnie.'

'Whereja live?'

'That way,' said Ronnie, pointing east. 'A hundred miles.'

'Geez! On a farm?'

'Yeah.'

There was another pause.

'You won't trade, then?'

'Dja go to school?'

'Sure,' said Gordie, looking surprised. 'Don't you?'

'I live too far.'

'Geez, you lucky stiff!'

Ronnie was so astounded by this remark that the goldie fell from his hand and almost got lost down the gear-shaft. He scrambled for it frantically and recovered it. The other

99

boy hung through the window and watched with held breath.

'You better trade. You'll only lose it.'

'But I want to keep it.'

'You'll lose it, sure. On a farm . . . it'll drop in the muck or a cow'll eat it.'

'We ain't got *cows!*' said Ronnie with a sudden snort of laughter.

'What have you got then?'

'Just wheat. And some hens.'

'They lay eggs?'

'Sure! Whatcha think we keep 'em for?'

'I dunno. Dja ever see a hen lay an egg?'

'Sure, millions of times.'

'I mean . . . You seen it comin' out?'

'Sure.'

'Sure must look funny.' The boy turned red, put his head down against the window-sill, and choked with laughter. Ronnie was puzzled and said nothing.

'Ronnie!'

Ronnie turned his head sharply at the sound of his father's peremptory call. Gordie lost his hold and fell backwards down the side of the truck. Hanging out of the window, Ronnie saw him spreadeagled in the mud. But he wasn't hurt. They caught each other's eyes and simultaneously burst out laughing.

Ronnie saw his father in the doorway of the store, a big box in his arms.

'Come and help your mother.'

He opened the door promptly and scrambled down backwards, jumping from the last stepping-place. Half on purpose, he tripped, and sat down in the mud beside Gordie. They were laughing so hysterically by now that neither of them could get up. Ronnie could feel the wet soaking through the seat of his trousers. It felt glorious – the cold, wicked touch of independence and freedom.

Then he felt something else – his father's big hand under his arm, hiking him to his feet.

'Get up from there! What do you think you're doing?'

'I fell, Pa!'

'You'll be in dutch when your mother sees the mess you're in. Get in the store now, and help her with the stuff.'

He ignored Gordie, still sprawling. Gordie was no concern of his.

With a pang of unease which was almost, but not quite, fear, Ronnie dashed into the store. His mother was there, helping the storeman to pack the last of the supplies into a box. He stopped still in the doorway and looked at her as if for the first time. Letting himself fall in the mud had, for the moment, put a distance between him and her; he noticed for the first time that her smooth, bunned hair was a little grey, that her face was rougher-looking and had much less colour in it than town women's. He noticed her clothes, the old, plain, faded dress which he had known since before he knew anything, longer now than other women's skirts, and different in other ways that he couldn't analyse. It hung down below her coat, which was relatively new, but still not pretty, only sensible and dark and warm. He looked at her whole figure and noticed it, too, was not like other women's, being big-boned, too tall, a little stooped. Ronnie stood open-mouthed with dismay, in the clarity of that moment of independent perception.

But it passed. She turned, and smiled at him, and it passed on the instant into the intimacy, almost one-ness, wherein she was, always had been and always would be so much a part of him that he didn't see her, any more than he saw his own nose.

'Here, take this box for me, will you, Ronnie?'

She pointed to a small box and he ran to pick it up. As he bent down he heard her gasp.

'Good grief, what've you been doing to yourself?'

'I fell, Mother.'

He dreaded her disapproval. He turned his face up and threw her a look of appeal. You never knew with her. She might be angry – every dirty garment had to be washed painfully by hand with a washboard and mangle, and drying was a problem in this damp season – or she might let it go,

101

either out of a flash of good nature and understanding, or just from sheer tiredness. Ronnie was lucky this time. Her rather grim face softened.

'Oh well . . . you're not often careless.'

He was deeply relieved. It was especially important to him that she shouldn't spoil today by scolding him. To thank her, he pressed his head against the warmth of her coat for a moment, then picked up the box and ran staggering with it to the door.

'Now don't go running with that, or you'll trip again.'

He slowed down and carried the box to the truck with conscientious slowness. As soon as his father had relieved him of it, and of his duty, he immediately looked round for Gordie. He couldn't see him, and his heart sank. He felt a strong sense of loss, and instinctively put his hands in his pockets to make sure the aggies were still there. They were. It was something more – even more – important that had gone.

But it hadn't, for as he and his mother and father settled themselves up in the high cabin of the truck, with him on the outside so he could fly his hand out of the window and feel the wind snatching at it on the way home, he caught sight of Gordie peeping round the edge of the store building. A great joy made a swelling inside his chest. He forgot himself completely and screamed, just as his father was switching on the engine:

'Gordie! C'm'ere!'

His mother looked round sharply – she seldom heard him yell, even with pain. Ronnie was beckoning wildly. The other boy, emboldened, ran to the side of the truck and hoisted himself up again.

'Here!'

Gordie held out his hand instantly, his face alive with happiness. Ronnie dropped the goldie into it. In another moment, the bird's-egg, with its glinting gold fragments, had been passed to him. The truck was just beginning to move. Gordie dropped off backwards, landing this time on his feet.

102

'Say, thanks a million!'

Ronnie waved and leant out of the window so far that his mother had to catch hold of the seat of his pants.

'See you in thirty days from now!' he yelled at the top of his lungs as the truck roared away from the kerb.

'Sure! See ya!'

Ronnie waved till Gordie was out of sight. Then he sank back into his narrow place. He heard, as if from far away, his mother warning him that he'd fall out and be killed if he kept leaning out of windows that way. After a while his father, with his eyes on the beginning of the long, straight road that would lead them home, asked:

'Who was that, anyway?'

'My friend,' answered Ronnie, looking at the horizon.

Follow On

The Short Story

What is a short story?

Horror, families, myths, science fiction, sport, neighbours, mystery, travel, school, love, ghosts, Westerns – almost any subject you can think of has been written about in one short story or another. Today the short story is one of the most popular forms of writing used by professional authors, and many are made into plays and films for television and the cinema.

A short story can vary in length from just a few hundred words to as many as 10,000. In this volume 'How The Elephant Became' is roughly 2,000 words while 'The Aggie Match' stretches to over 9,000 words. When asked what is typical about a short story Roald Dahl wrote: 'There is no time for the sun shining through the pine trees'. What he meant was that the short story writer has to throw the reader right into the action. There is no time to set the scene in the way a full-length novel does. With the stories in this book, it is usually the action which is more important than the setting or the characters, though of course all are important.

Talking about short stories

When you are talking about short stories it is useful to know the meaning of certain basic 'technical' words which are used whether you are discussing a short story, a novel or a play.

Plot
The plot refers to the *action* in a story. All of us read through a story because we want to know what happens next and how it will end. Look at 'The Hitch-hiker' for an example of a tale in which we keep reading because we want to find out just what the hitch-hiker does for his living.

Characters

These are the *'inhabitants'* of the stories. They may be 'finger-smiths', ghosts, young children, animals, teachers or parents. Sometimes characters are described in great detail; at other times, they are only sketched very briefly. And writers often want us to take sides for or against their characters. Think of some examples of *how* characters are written about in these stories.

Setting

This word refers to the *place or period* of time in which the story is set. As with the characters, it is something which the writer can either hint at briefly or describe in great detail. For example, compare the settings and how the authors describe them in 'The Aggie Match' and 'The Choice Is Yours'.

Narrator

Of course it is the author – Bernard Ashley, Merle Hodge or Jan Mark – who actually writes the words, but all stories are told from a particular *point of view*.

The writer can do one of the following:

1. Pretend to be in the shoes of one of the characters in the story and see everything through that character's eyes. This means that the story will be told using 'I'. And this is called 'first-person narration'.
2. Stand outside the action and look down on it, seeing everything that happens to everyone. Characters are referred to as 'he' or 'she' or 'it'. This is called 'third-person narration'.

Which stories in this collection are told using the 'first-person narrator', and which use the 'third-person narrator'?

Themes

Writers write to tell a story. We read to find out 'what happens next'. But stories often have important *ideas or messages* in them. These are known as themes. Lynne Reid Banks in 'The Aggie Match' is writing as much about friendship as she is about a boy and his games with marbles. Jan Mark is telling us something about teachers and rules in 'The Choice Is Yours'. What other themes can you find in this book?

Style

This is something very difficult to define but generally refers to the *way* in which a writer tells the story and brings together characters, plot, setting and theme – in other words, all the ingredients of the story. A ghost story will be told in a different way from a love story, and all writers have their own habits and tricks of style.

When you are talking about the styles of writers in this book think about some of the following:
- length of sentences and paragraphs. A writer may use longer sentences for detailed descriptions of landscape, but short, sharp sentences when wanting to create tension or suspense.
- attention to detail. For example, look at how Gene Kemp describes Dawn Taylor's 'perfect Cupid's bow mouth'.
- how the writer sets the mood and atmosphere of the tale.
- the opening and closing sentences of a story. Does the writer save up a surprise ending?
- how the writer makes us laugh.
- where the writer wants us to focus our attention and who s/he wants us to take sides with.
- the use of conversations and dialogue.
- the use of language generally; for example, Hans in 'The Last Laugh'.

Writing your own short story

Plan out your own story by asking and answering the following questions:
1. What is going to be the *subject* of the story?
2. Where is it going to take place? Are there going to be several different places?
3. How many characters are there going to be?
4. Are you going to use the *first* or the *third*-person narration?
5. Are there any particular ideas or themes you want to put across to your reader?
6. Are you going to have lots of dialogue, detailed descriptions, humour, suspense, or what?
    Also ask yourself the question: *Who* am I writing for?

A plan for writing
1. Jot down your ideas for the story.
2. Sort out roughly how many paragraphs you'll need. How long will the story be?
3. Write out your story in rough.

4. Ask somebody to read it through with you. How can it be made better?
5. Rewrite the story, paying careful attention to spelling, sentences and paragraphs.
6. Read it over once more to see that you haven't made any silly mistakes.

Before you start your writing you might like to read the following words of advice from the famous short story writer Roald Dahl.

Here are some of the qualities you should possess or should try to acquire if you wish to become a fiction writer:

1 You should have a lively imagination.
2 You should be able to write well. By that I mean you should be able to make a scene come alive in the reader's mind. Not everybody has this ability. It is a gift, and you either have it or you don't.
3 You must have stamina. In other words, you must be able to stick to what you are doing and never give up, for hour after hour, day after day, week after week and month after month.
4 You must be a perfectionist. That means you must never be satisfied with what you have written until you have re-written it again and again, making it as good as you possibly can.
5 You must have strong self-discipline. You are working alone. No one is employing you. No one is around to give you the sack if you don't turn up for work, or to tick you off if you start slacking.
6 It helps a lot if you have a keen sense of humour. This is not essential when writing for grown-ups, but for children, it's vital.
7 You must have a degree of humility. The writer who thinks that his work is marvellous is heading for trouble.

Roald Dahl (from *Lucky Break*)

GOOD LUCK WITH YOUR WRITING!

May Queen

About the story
This story, and *Joe's Cat*, are taken from a collection of short stories by Gene Kemp called *Dog Days and Cat Naps*. Here, she writes about both stories:

It sounds obvious to say that all stories are different – of course they are or we wouldn't bother to read them – but what I mean is that they do arrive on the page in different ways.

Take the two stories from *Dog Days and Cat Naps* for instance. *Joe's Cat* arrived in my head all of a piece when I woke up one morning . . . *May Queen* took longer than *Joe's Cat*, and I had to put it together much more carefully. Lizzie, of all my characters, is the one I identify with, even to the specs and teeth. The bottomless pond, and Dawn, Lizzie's beautiful but dim friend, were part of my childhood. I wrote this story very carefully, rewriting and rewriting and never sure whether it was worth putting in the collection.

If *Joe's Cat* was inspiration, *May Queen* was perspiration, but now five years later I think *May Queen* is the better story of the two.

(Gene Kemp writes more about the story *Joe's Cat* on page 116)

Points for Discussion or Writing
1. Dawn Taylor has 'a perfect Cupid's bow mouth'. What does this mean? Find out who Cupid was in Roman legend.
2. What is the May Queen festival? Find out about it.
3. What does Lizzie Barnes think of Dawn Taylor?
4. How is Dawn feeling as she prepares for the festival?
5. Why is Joan not interested in all the preparations?
6. 'This pond had atmosphere. This pond had mystery' (page 2). What *exactly is* different about this pond from the other one on Farmer Woolley's land?
7. 'We climbed a tree to see if there were any Palefaces lurking' (page 3). Why does Lizzie use the word 'Palefaces'?
8. Why do Lizzie and Jeff tell Dawn that the pond is enchanted?
9. Why do you think Dawn just bursts into laughter when she falls into the pond?
10. What are Lizzie's feelings at the end of the story?

Ideas for Writing
- Write a story about another adventure involving Lizzie, Dawn, Jeff and Farmer Woolley.
- Rewrite this story imagining that Dawn tells it.
- Describe the full events of the May Queen festival.
- Think of a time when you or one of your friends was involved in an accident like Dawn's. Tell the story. You can make this real or imaginary.

Further Reading
Gene Kemp is a well-known writer for children. This story you will find with many others about animals and children in *Dog Days and Cat Naps*. You might also like to read these novels by the same author: *The Turbulent Term of Tyke Tiler* and *Gowie Corby Plays Chicken*. Another short story of hers, 'The Rescue of Karen Arscott', is included in the collection called *School's O.K.*

The Last Laugh

About the story
Gervase Phinn writes:

> This story is based on a true incident which happened when I taught English to foreign pupils in a Language School. Hans was typical of many pupils who came to this country for the first time with a very clear, but quite false, picture of what English people were like. He was disappointed to find that I didn't wear a bowler hat or carry an umbrella everywhere, that I didn't have a 'stiff upper lip' and that I didn't talk in proverbs.

Points for Discussion or Writing
1. What sort of a person is Miss Sculthorpe? Do you think the pupils like her?
2. Why does Jason Johnson get his name mentioned so often?
3. What sort of language mistakes does Hans make?
4. Why doesn't Hans write about the shells?
5. What does Hans think 'proper' English is?
6. Hans mentions some proverbs. Think up some examples for when each of the proverbs might be correctly used.
7. Why does Miss Sculthorpe say to Hans, 'When in Rome you do as the Romans do'?

109

8. Why does Hans smile for the first time in assembly?
9. As the story ends, what *is* John Mullarkey laughing at?
10. Do you think Hans would have got away with his 'prayer' at your school? What might have caught him out?

Ideas for Writing

● This story is all about differences between languages. Make a list of the different languages spoken by pupils in your class. You could also tape record some examples of different dialects and accents.

● Different countries have their own proverbs. For example, the Chinese say:

> Give someone a fish and you've fed them for a day.
> Teach them to fish and you've fed them for life.

And in 'Sharlo's Strange Bargain' there is the proverb: 'Shutmout' no ketch fly'. Find out and note down as many proverbs as you can from other countries.

● Write a story called: 'The Assembly That Went Wrong'.

● Write about a time when a pupil embarrassed a teacher but the teacher didn't know about it. This can be a real or imaginary story.

● Like Hans, many English people have a 'false picture' of what people in other countries are really like. Write a short piece, either funny or sad, in which misunderstandings occur on a first visit abroad.

Further Reading

There are many stories and novels about school-life. If you don't already know them, you might like to try the novels of Robert Leeson: *The Third Class Genie* and the various 'Grange Hill' books. *The Goalkeeper's Revenge* by Bill Naughton, *Summer's End* by Archie Hill, *Cider With Rosie* by Laurie Lee and *The Fib and Other Stories* by George Layton – all have enjoyable accounts of school days.

Jeffie Lemmington And Me

About the story
Merle Hodge writes about her life and work, and how this has influenced her writing:

I was born and brought up in Trinidad, and went to university in London. For much of my working life I have been involved with children: I worked in a children's home/residential school in Denmark; as an *au pair* in Paris and London; and as a teacher in secondary schools in Trinidad. Between 1979 and 1983 I worked in the Grenada Revolution, and was closely involved in developing new programmes in education.

In all the stories that I have written so far, I look at the world through the eyes of children. I enjoy getting children to punch holes in the airtight falsehoods that adults weave around themselves, like race and class prejudice, and all forms of pompousness. Remember 'The King's New Clothes' by Hans Christian Anderson . . .?

Points for Discussion or Writing
1. What do we learn about the boy who tells the story from the opening paragraphs?
2. What is his reaction to the sight of snow?
3. Why does he use the phrase 'Up There'?
4. What reasons does the boy give for wanting to return to Granny and Uncle Nello?
5. What do the two boys like about being together?
6. Why do you think Jeffie Lemmington is told not to play with the narrator?
7. Why do the boys decide to run away? Where do they plan to go?
8. What things frighten them on their journey?
9. What tells you that the boys made the most of their adventure once they returned to school?
10. How do the events of the story and, in particular, the ending change the parents' feelings towards the boys being together?

Ideas for Writing
- Write a story in which someone, or a group of people, are prejudiced against someone else.
- Imagine you decided to run away from home for some reason with a friend. Write the story of what happened.
- Write out the scene in which Jeffie and Me tell their adventure to friends back at school. Now act it out.
- 'A fearful thundering . . . and the giant centipede rushed in' (page 21). Use this as a starting point for a story.

Further Reading
Merle Hodge writes mostly about children. You might also like to read 'Millicent' in *Over Our Way*, an anthology of short stories written by Caribbean authors. Slightly older readers would enjoy her novel, *Crick Crack, Monkey*.

How The Elephant Became

About the story
This story belongs to a well-known collection called *How the Whale Became*. Just how human beings, animals and Nature were created or have evolved has been the subject of many stories throughout history. Writers like Ted Hughes have offered unusual and amusing accounts of the Creation. The opening of *How the Whale Became* reads: 'To begin with, all the creatures were pretty much alike – very different from what they are now. They had no idea what they were going to become'. In this story it is Bombo who finds his purpose in the animal kingdom.

Points for Discussion or Writing
1. At the start of the story, why is Bombo 'the unhappiest of all the creatures'?
2. Why does Bombo envy the Buffalo?
3. Why do the other creatures laugh at him?
4. Which animal first notices the forest fire?
5. Why do the animals fear that there will be no escape from the fire?
6. How does Bombo keep himself cool?
7. How does he save all the other animals?
8. Why do the animals not crown him as their king?
9. How many different creatures are mentioned in the story? Make a list of them.
10. If you were a God looking down on all the animals you had created, which ones would you be most pleased with, and why?

Ideas for Writing
● Write your own story called: 'Forest Fire'. You can include human beings as well as animals.
● Choose any animal you admire and write the story of its

creation. Try to make it original and, perhaps, amusing. You will find lots of good ideas in *How the Whale Became*.

● Different peoples and cultures throughout history have had their own stories about creation. Put together a project which compares the various Creation Myths. Here are some ideas to get you started:

Creation Myths

The Indian Myth of Creation

At first there was no earth and sky; there were only two great eggs. But they were no ordinary eggs for they were soft and shone like gold. As the eggs went round in space they collided and broke open. From one half came the earth and from the other half came the sky. The sky took the earth to be his wife. But the earth was too big for the sky to hold in his arms so he said to her, 'Though you are my wife you are bigger than I. Make yourself smaller.' The earth accordingly made herself smaller and as she became smaller the mountains and valleys were formed. And the earth and the sky were married and made every kind of tree and grass and all living creatures.

The Egyptian Myth of Creation

Long ago there was nothing but sea and darkness. One day a flower grew out of the sea. The flower opened to reveal a scarab beetle which gave off light. And so the darkness became light. The beetle changed into a man called Ra. Ra was king of the universe. Ra was lonely so he spat out a son called Shu and a daughter called Tefnut. One day Ra lost his children in the sea. He searched for them and when he at last found them he cried for joy. From out of his tears, men grew. That is why in the Egyptian language the word for 'man' is the same as the word for 'tear'.

The Babylonian Myth of Creation

Babylonia was an ancient kingdom in Southern Mesopotamia. It lay between the rivers Tigris and Euphrates. This country is now called Iraq. The Babylonians believed that their world was created when a good god called Marduk captured an evil goddess called Tiamet. He trapped her in a net and then strangled her. Marduk cut Tiamet's body in two. From the top half he made the skies and the bottom half became the Earth. After this, everything that was good in life was thought to have been caused by Marduk. The evil

and disasters that happened were blamed on Tiamet. Just as
Marduk and Tiamet fought, so men will always struggle between
leading a good life and leading a bad life.

Further Reading

Ted Hughes is one of our most famous living poets. He has also
written a lot of poetry and prose especially for children. Perhaps
his best-known book is the fabulous tale of *The Iron Man*. You may
also like to read his clever short story 'The Tigerboy' (available in
The Storyteller 2, edited by Barrett & Morpurgo) and a volume of
plays *The Coming of the Kings*. His collections of poetry for
children include: *Meet My Folks!*, *Season Songs*, *Moon-Bells*, and
Under The North Star.

Sharlo's Strange Bargain

About the story

Ralph Prince writes about his life and work, and about the story:

I was born in Antigua, a small island in the Caribbean. I have
lived and worked in several Caribbean countries and in Great
Britain. I have also travelled extensively in Europe and the
USA.

It has been my good fortune to have done various kinds of
work, which I regard as having been an important part of my
education. These have included the following: school-teacher,
labourer, clerk, news-correspondent, freelance journalist,
editor, insurance salesman, photographer, Spanish translator-
and-interpreter, and lecturer.

The story 'Sharlo's Strange Bargain' is read in schools
throughout the Caribbean and schoolchildren have often asked
me if the story really happened. My usual answer is, 'I wonder
about that myself too'. It probably had its origin in stories I used
to hear as a boy, of people who suddenly got rich because (or so it
was said) they 'made a deal with the devil'.

As far as I remember, my story is largely from my imagination, but with a West Indian flavour.

Some words in this story may be unfamiliar to you. Here is a short glossary:

Ackee A vegetable found in the Caribbean, often served with saltfish.

Calabash A pot or container made from the hard shell of a tropical fruit.

Calaloo A green vegetable often used in soups and stews.

Fungee A dish of vegetables, served with saltfish.

Obeah Witchcraft.

Pepperpot A highly seasoned soup or stew.

Souse A dish made from pigs' trotters, usually cooked with onions and vinegar.

Points for Discussion or Writing
1. After reading the first paragraph of the story, what did you expect it to be about?
2. For what two things was Sharlo famous in his village?
3. 'The man seemed neither young nor old, but ageless' (page 30). Does this description give any clue as to the man's identity?
4. What else are we told about the man which might help us guess who he is? Look carefully at page 30.
5. Why doesn't Sharlo want to part with his fife?
6. How does the man persuade Sharlo to swap the fife for the calabash?
7. What effect does owning the calabash have on Sharlo?
8. 'Shut-mout' no ketch fly'. What does Sharlo mean?
9. Why does Sharlo finally give food to Zakky?
10. Why was Sharlo never seen again?

Ideas for Writing
- Write a story called: 'The Devil's Den' *or* 'A Pact with the Devil'.
- Imagine you are Sharlo. Tell the story of what happened to you the night after you told your secret to Zakky.
- A year later Zakky strikes a similar bargain with the Devil. Write the story.
- What other legends or stories do you know about people making bargains with the Devil? Write one of them. Act out the legend if you like.

Further Reading

You can read more stories by Ralph Prince in *Jewels of the Sun*. His short story, 'The Water Woman and her Lover' is published in the anthology *Over Our Way*.

If you want to read more stories from the Caribbean, try these anthologies: *The Sun's Eye*, *West Indian Narrative*, and *Caribbean Narrative*.

Joe's Cat

About the story
Gene Kemp writes:

> *Joe's Cat* arrived in my head all of a piece when I woke up one morning. Just before then I'd read about a cat haunting a house, a friendly animal, brushing people's legs with its tail and I liked that. I've always enjoyed fairy tales and the cheeky cat in Puss in Boots appealed to me, and I could just see him with big furry legs instead of the boots. Finally, I remembered having to leave the country to live in the town and I missed it very much for a long time. So these three elements all churned together and came out as *Joe's Cat*.

(On page 108, you can read what Gene Kemp feels about the writing of this story and *May Queen*, both of which come from the collection *Dog Days and Cat Naps*.)

Points for Discussion or Writing
1. Why is Joe happy at the beginning of the story?
2. What are Joe's favourite sports?
3. Where does the cat get its name Boots from? What is its special toy?
4. 'There were two Joes, he sometimes thought' (page 37). What does Joe mean?
5. Why do Joe and his mother have to move house when his father dies?
6. What does Joe dislike about his new school?
7. How does life in the city affect and change him?
8. Why does Joe travel out to his old home?
9. In what ways does Boots help Joe in the course of the story?
10. What do you understand by the last paragraph of the story?

Ideas for Writing
- Write another adventure in which Joe is 'rescued' by Boots.
- Joe obviously finds it difficult when he moves from country to city. Make a list of the advantages and disadvantages – as you see them – of living in the country and the city.
- 'Joe picked up his pen, and the sights and smells and sounds of the farmyard came to him so vividly that the words flowed out of his head and poured down the page' (page 42). Write the story Joe told that day in class.
- Write a story called: 'School. School. Failure. Misery.'
- Write a story about an animal haunting a house. It can be friendly, like Boots in this story, or unfriendly.

Lenny's Red-Letter Day

About the story
Bernard Ashley writes:

> Every school has a 'flea-bag', it seems to be a sad fact of life, and Lenny is one of them. He isn't a real person I know but a mix of the features of many. Writers are like that, they don't copy characters but create them: that way the characters have a larger appeal, a universality, which would be missing in a clone. Also, writers – and especially doctor/writers, teacher/writers, lawyer/writers – must always be wary of betraying professional knowledge and confidences. So 'Lenny' is 'Lenny' and *no one* else, but a lot of other people I've known.
>
> In the story, as the God-like author, I went some way towards solving Lenny's problem for a while. What stories we'd write if real-life problems could be solved the way fictitious problems are!

Points For Discussion or Writing
1. What do we learn about Lenny Fraser in the opening paragraphs of the story?
2. Where does the phrase 'Red-Letter Day' come from?
3. The narrator says it would have been better if Miss Blake hadn't noticed it was Lenny's birthday. Why does he say this?
4. What do Prakash's parents do for a living?

117

5. Why does Prakash keep 'the other eye on the clock' all the time that he and Lenny are playing Monopoly?
6. How does Nalini react when she sees Lenny? What does Prakash think of her behaviour?
7. 'Didn't Miss Banks once say something about leopards never changing their spots?' (page 48). Why does Prakash remember this after Lenny has gone home?
8. What kind of a person does Lenny's mum seem to be?
9. How does Prakash feel at the end of the day's events?
10. 'It was as if he was trying to tell me something' (page 51). What was Lenny trying to say to Prakash?

Ideas For Writing

● Write another story about Lenny, Prakash and Nalini. Perhaps in this story they all get on well together?
● Write a story titled: 'A Case of Mistaken Identity'.
● Imagine you are Lenny Fraser. Write down what you think about school and the children in your class.
● Think of a time when someone in *your* class was treated badly by the other children. Write the story. It can be real or imaginary. Does it have a happy or serious ending?

Further Reading

You can read other short stories about the children in this story in a book called *I'm Trying to Tell You* by Bernard Ashley. His popular story 'Equal Rights' is available in *Openings*. Bernard Ashley has written several novels for children which you may like to read: *The Trouble with Donovan Croft*, *Terry on the Fence*, *A Kind of Wild Justice*, *Break in the Sun*, *Dodgem*, and *All My Men*.

The Hitch-hiker

About the story

Roald Dahl is famous for his funny and often strange books for children like *Charlie and the Chocolate Factory* and *Fantastic Mr Fox*. But he has also written many short stories for older readers. Have you ever wondered where he gets all his ideas from? He says that good original plots are hard to come by but can come to you at any moment:

You never know when a lovely idea is going to flit suddenly into your mind, but by golly, when it does come along, you grab it with both hands and hang on to it tight. The trick is to write it down at once, otherwise you'll forget it. A good plot is like a dream. If you don't write down your dream on paper the moment you wake up, the chances are you'll forget it and it'll be gone forever. (From *Lucky Break*)

When you are reading this story, think about where Roald Dahl might have got his ideas and plot from. Is Dahl himself the driver of the big BMW? Did he really meet a strange hitch-hiker? Or did he fall victim to a skilful pickpocket?

Points for Discussion or Writing

1. Why does the narrator stop to pick up the hitch-hiker? What reasons does he give?
2. Where is the hitch-hiker going and why?
3. Why does the hitch-hiker think the driver of the car must be a good writer?
4. What makes the driver decide to test the top speed of the car?
5. What attitude does the policeman take when he starts speaking to the driver and hitch-hiker?
6. What are the reactions of the driver and the hitch-hiker to the policeman's questions? Are they the same?
7. What is the first clue to the hitch-hiker's real trade?
8. Why does the hitch-hiker call himself a 'fingersmith' rather than a 'pickpocket'?
9. Why might the hitch-hiker be described as a kind of Robin Hood?
10. Why won't the narrator be reported for speeding?

Ideas for Writing

- 'The secret of life is to become very very good at somethin' that's very very 'ard to do' (page 54). Write a story using these words as your starting point.
- Imagine you are the fingersmith. Write a story, from your point of view, about another of your adventures.
- Write out the scene when the narrator arrives home and tells his family about the hitch-hiker and the policeman. Act out the scene if you like.

- Write a short story using one of these titles:
  A Day at the Races
  The Hitch-hiker
  The Police Siren
  A Peculiar Trade

Further Reading
Among Roald Dahl's many books for children are: *Charlie and the Chocolate Factory*, *Danny, the Champion of the World*, *James and the Giant Peach*, *The Magic Finger*, and *Charlie and the Great Glass Elevator*. 'The Hitch-hiker' is included with eight more bizarre and intriguing stories in *A Roald Dahl Selection*.

The Choice Is Yours

About the story
Jan Mark writes:

My mother was a nuisance at school, so was I and so was my daughter. It's a family tradition in the female line. We were in trouble most of the time for one thing or another, but occasionally it wasn't our fault. My mother used to tell me that she once spent a whole afternoon carrying messages between two teachers who were having a row, and I remember being faced with the problem of having to be in two places at once for two different teachers, neither of whom would give way to the other. I forget what happened in the end but when I wrote *The Choice Is Yours* I ran the two incidents together, with embellishments.

Points for Discussion or Writing
1. What sort of people are Miss Francis and Miss Taylor? How do they treat pupils generally?
2. How do they react to Brenda in this story?
3. 'Miss Francis sighed a sigh that turned a page on the music stand' (page 67). What does this sentence tell us about Miss Francis's mood?
4. How does Miss Francis show her lack of interest in sport?
5. Why do you think neither teacher will begin their practice until Brenda is present?

120

6. 'It's a matter of principle' (page 72). What does Miss Francis mean?
7. 'The tears of self-pity turned hot with anger' (page 73). What mood is Brenda in at this point in the story?
8. 'The prodigal returns' (page 73). Why does Miss Francis use this phrase?
9. Why does Brenda come to the decision she does? What would *you* have done in her place? Who do you sympathise with in the story?
10. 'There was no rule against that' (page 74). Why does the story end with these words, do you think?

Ideas for Writing
● Write about a time when you, like Brenda, were put in a difficult position by teachers at school. It could have been about making a choice or about telling on a friend.
● This story is all about rules. Make a list of your school rules. Then make a list of those rules that you would abolish. Give reasons why.
● Imagine you are Brenda. You go to the headteacher to complain about the way you've been treated. Write the scene, and then act it.
● Miss Francis and Miss Taylor meet in the staff-room and start arguing about Brenda. Write the scene. Act it out.

Further Reading
Jan Mark has written many stories for and about young people. This story comes from a collection of short stories called *Nothing To Be Afraid Of*, a volume peopled with strange and cunning characters. Two longer school stories are to be found in *Hairs In The Palm Of The Hand*. You might also like to read 'Do You Read Me?' in *School's O.K.*. Her novels include: *Thunder and Lightnings* and *Under the Autumn Garden*.

The Toad

About the story
Melanie Bush was fifteen and attending school in Manchester when she wrote this story. It won a prize in the 1982 W.H. Smith

Young Writers' Competition, a competition which received more than 33,000 entries from writers aged six to sixteen. She begins the story by saying that she has just finished reading a book called *Metamorphosis* in which a man wakes up one morning to find himself turned into a giant insect. From then on, the insect is the narrator. Melanie Bush isn't the animal in her own story but her father *is*. 'The Toad' is a funny but also slightly disturbing tale which makes us look at human beings from a different point of view than our usual one.

Points for Discussion or Writing
1. What is the first thing which makes the writer think that the Toad is indeed her father?
2. What are her mother's first reactions to the news that the Toad is Dad?
3. 'I have put two and two together . . .'
   'And got five' (page 76). What does the brother mean when he interrupts?
4. What are the brother's reactions to the narrator's thoughts about the Toad?
5. 'John and I seemed to be the optimists and my elder brother and mother were the realists' (page 79). Explain the meaning of this.
6. In what ways does Mum's mood change in the course of the story?
7. Why do you think Mum changes her mind about the Toad?
8. 'The day Mum trod on the toad was the day Dad returned home' (page 82). What do you understand by this ending?
9. Why might Melanie Bush have written this story?
10. Look up the word 'metamorphosis'. What is its real meaning?

Ideas for Writing
- Imagine you wake up one day to find yourself turned into an animal. Write your story under the title 'A Day In The Life Of . . .'
- Think of a time when something happened in your family which led to a split of views. Write about it.
- 'I have put two and two together . . and got five.' Use this as the starting point for a story.
- Imagine the scene when Dad returns home at the end of the

story. The rest of the family try to explain about the Toad. Write
what happens. Act out the scene.

Further Reading
More and more examples of good writing from young people are
being published in book form. The W.H. Smith Young Writers'
Competition is held annually and a collection of award-winning
entries is published. You might also like to look at *Our Lives*
(ILEA English Centre) and *Hey, Mr Butterfly* for some fine
examples of young writers.

The Aggie Match

About the story
Lynne Reid Banks writes:

> I spent my early teenage years on the Canadian prairies and got a
> feeling of the loneliness of some of the remote farms we occa-
> sionally passed while travelling from one big town to another.
> The actual aggie match was based on the games of marbles I
> remember so well from my five prairie springs. I wrote the story
> in 1975, many years after leaving Canada – thirty, to be exact! –
> in a sudden, deep fit of nostalgia. It was quite unrelated to any
> other story I've ever written and even as I was writing it, felt as if
> it were coming from somewhere outside me.

Points for Discussion or Writing
1. Ronnie begins each day by running to look out of his window
   for passing cars. Why does he do this?
2. Why does Ronnie want to go to school?
3. Why does Ronnie look forward so much to Town-days?
4. What strikes him most about watching other children in the
   town? How are they unlike him?
5. Explain the rules of the aggie match.
6. What gives Ronnie his 'first taste of power'?
7. What shows that Ronnie has never played the game of marbles
   before?
8. Why does Ronnie deliberately fall into the mud alongside
   Gordie?

9. Towards the end of the story, Ronnie notices something about his mother which he has never seen before. Why does this happen? What does he see in her?
10. ' "My friend", answered Ronnie, looking at the horizon' (page 103). Why do you think the story ends in this way?

Ideas for Writing
- Write a story about the next time Ronnie visits the town and meets up with Gordie.
- Imagine Ronnie persuades his parents to let Gordie come to their farm for a short visit. Describe what happens during his stay.
- Write a story about a time when you've felt very alone.
- Some other story titles:
  The Competition/The Return Match
  Making Friends
  Town Versus Country Life
  My Treasured Possession

Further Reading
Lynne Reid Banks has written several novels for young people. They include: *One More River, The Farthest-Away Mountain, The Indian in the Cupboard, I, Houdini, The Writing on the Wall,* and *Maura's Angel.* Her short story 'Trust' is published in *The Real Thing*, an anthology of romantic stories.

Ideas for group and individual work

You can talk about these ideas in groups or put together a project on the short story.

+ Which of the stories did you enjoy most? Give your reasons. Write a short review of your favourite story from this collection which will make other people want to read it. Try to comment on *plot, themes, characters, style,* and *setting* (see pages 104–105).

+ Which characters did you like or identify with? Write your own story about one of these characters. Or bring together characters from different stories – maybe a story with Lizzie Barnes and Brenda; and one with Lenny Fraser and Ronnie?

+ What are your reactions to the ways the stories end? If you don't like one of the endings, try rewriting or acting out a different one.

+ Take the last lines of any of the stories and write some scenes that might follow on. Act them out in groups.

+ Some of the authors have tried to bring out the humour and fun of events and characters in their stories. Look back over them and talk about where and how they have succeeded in doing this. 'The Last Laugh' is perhaps the best place to begin.

+ Bernard Ashley in 'Lenny's Red-Letter Day' uses the first-person 'I' narration, while in 'Sharlo's Strange Bargain' Ralph Prince has a third-person narrator observing the action from the outside.
Which type of narrator is used in each of the twelve stories? What seem to you the advantages and disadvantages of the different types?
Rewrite one of the stories, changing the narrator. For example, you could retell 'Lenny's Red-Letter Day' from *Lenny's* point of view.

+ As well as telling a story, writers often want to make us think carefully about an idea or a theme.

What ideas or themes have you come across in these stories? Have any of the stories made you think about a subject – like loneliness or friendship – which you have not thought about before?

Have they changed your opinions about anything?

+ When we write a story we often base it on something we have seen or done ourselves. If someone writes a book about himself or herself it's called an 'autobiography'. Think about these stories. Do you think any of them really happened to the writers? Are any of them autobiographical? Look again at what Bernard Ashley writes on page 117.

+ Some of the stories are about the relationships between children and teachers, or children and their parents. Do they seem realistic to you?

+ Four of the stories are set in schools. Think about what makes a good *school story*. What do you need to include? Write your own tale about schooldays.

Put together your own short story anthology

Look back over the stories in this collection. They have different settings, themes, styles and characters. There are examples of fables, school stories, country tales, fantasy and perhaps auto-biography. Now put together your own collection.

Begin by retelling one of the stories in *Round Two*. Try to include five or six different types of story: ones about sport or love or ghosts or perhaps a Western.

Design an eye-catching cover for your anthology. The school library might like your finished book to put on the shelves for other pupils to read.

Write a play

Choose one of the short stories and turn it into a play-script for acting. This is quite simple to do:

+ Read through the story a few times.
+ Pick out just a few scenes if you don't want to retell the whole story.
+ Work through each page slowly, editing where necessary.
+ Put the speaker's name in the margin.
+ Every word that he or she *speaks* goes on the main part of the page.

+ You *don't* need speech marks.
+ Details of each speaker's reactions, feelings or movements need to be written as stage directions. Remember to use the present tense.
+ When you have finished, read your play through to see that it flows easily.
+ Tape it. Present it to the rest of your class.

Here is a short example done for you. It is taken from 'The Last Laugh' (page 8):

Scene	A classroom
Characters	Miss Sculthorpe, Valerie, Martin, Micky, Hans

Miss Sculthorpe enters the classroom smiling broadly.

MISS S   Will you all look this way, please? And that includes you, Jason Johnson. Thank you. Now this morning we have a new addition to our class. (*Turning towards Hans*) This is Hans.

VALERIE   Where's he from, Miss?

MISS S   I'm just about to tell you, Valerie dear, if you'll let me finish.

Hans stands in front of the class making no expression.

MISS S   Can anyone guess which country Hans comes from? His name should give you a clue.

MARTIN   Is he from Ireland, Miss? My cousin's from Ireland and she's got a funny name.

MISS S   (*strict*) Hans is not a funny name, Martin. In fact it's quite a common name in his country.

MARTIN   Miss, my cousin's name's Attracta.

MICKY   (*interrupting*) Blimey! Fancy calling somebody a tractor! What's her brother called – a combine harvester?

MARTIN   (*spluttering*) No! Not a tractor like the one you drive round a farm. It's all one word – Attracta. Twit!

Note
Start with something quite easy with just two or three speakers, before going on to something more complicated. It also helps to

127

choose a story in which there is plenty of dialogue!
Scenes to start you off:

a. The Wonderland scene in 'May Queen' (pages 3–6)
b. Sharlo meets the devil in 'Sharlo's Strange Bargain' (pages 30–32)
c. The hitch-hiker and car-driver in 'The Hitch-hiker', before the arrival of the policeman (pages 52–55)
d. Any scene in 'The Toad'.

Further Reading

Note: Where a book is published in both hardback and paperback editions, details of paperback only are given.

May Queen
Joe's Cat
Gene Kemp, short stories – *Dog Days and Cat Naps*, Puffin, 1983; 'The Rescue of Karen Arscott' in *School's O.K.*, Unwin Hyman Short Stories, Unwin Hyman, 1984; novels – *The Turbulent Term of Tyke Tiler*, Puffin, 1979; *Gowie Corby Plays Chicken*, Puffin 1981

The Last Laugh
Robert Leeson, *The Third Class Genie*, Armada, 1975; *Grange Hill Rules – O.K.?*, Armada, 1979; *Grange Hill Goes Wild*, Armada, 1980; *Grange Hill for Sale*, Armada, 1981; *Grange Hill Home and Away*, Armada, 1983
Bill Naughton, *The Goalkeeper's Revenge and Other Stories*, New Windmill Series, Heinemann Educational Books, 1967
Archie Hill, *Summer's End*, Wheaton, 1979
Laurie Lee, *Cider with Rosie*, Penguin, 1970
George Layton, *The Fib and Other Stories*, Knockouts Series, Longman, 1979

Jeffie Lemmington And Me
Merle Hodge, *Crick-Crack, Monkey*, Caribbean Writers' Series, Heinemann Educational Books, 1981; 'Millicent' in *Over Our Way*, edited by Jean D'Costa and Velma Pollard, Longman Caribbean, 1980

How The Elephant Became
Ted Hughes, *How the Whale Became and Other Stories*, Puffin, 1971; *The Iron Man: A Story in Five Nights*, Faber, 1971; 'The Tigerboy' in *The Storyteller Book 2*, ed. Michael Morpurgo and

Graham Barrett, Ward Lock Educational, 1980; *The Coming of the Kings and Other Plays*, Faber, 1976; *Moon-bells and Other Poems*, Chatto, 1978; *Under the North Star*, Faber, 1981

Sharlo's Strange Bargain
Ralph Prince, *Jewels of the Sun*, Nelson, 1979; 'The Waterwoman and her Lover' in *Over Our Way*, edited by Jean D'Costa and Velma Pollard, Longman Caribbean, 1980
Anthologies of stories from the Caribbean – *The Sun's Eye*, compiled by Anne Walmsley, Longman Caribbean, 1968; *West Indian Narrative*, by Kenneth Ramchand, Nelson, 1980; *Caribbean Narrative*, edited by O.R. Dathorne, Heinemann Educational, 1966

Lenny's Red Letter Day
Bernard Ashley: novels *The Trouble With Donovan Croft*, Puffin Books, 1977; *Terry On The Fence*, Puffin, 1978; *A Kind of Wild Justice*, Puffin, 1982; *All My Men*, Puffin, 1979; *Break in the Sun*, Puffin, 1981; *Dodgem*, Puffin, 1983; short stories – *I'm Trying to Tell You*, Puffin, 1982; 'Equal Rights' in *Openings*, Unwin Hyman Short Stories, Unwin Hyman, 1982

The Hitch-hiker
Roald Dahl, *Charlie and the Chocolate Factory*, Puffin, 1973; *Danny the Champion of the World*, Puffin, 1977; *James and the Giant Peach*, Puffin, 1973; *The Magic Finger*, Puffin, 1974; *Charlie and the Great Glass Elevator*, Puffin, 1975; *A Roald Dahl Selection*, edited by Roy Blatchford, Longman Imprint Books, 1980

The Choice Is Yours
Jan Mark, short stories – 'Do You Read Me?' in *School's O.K.*, Unwin Hyman Short Stories, Unwin Hyman, 1984; *Nothing To Be Afraid Of*, Puffin, 1982; *Hairs in the Palm of the Hand*, Kestrel, 1981; novels – *Thunder and Lightnings*, Puffin, 1978, *Under the Autumn Garden*, Puffin, 1980.

The Toad

Young Writers One – 23rd Year of the Children as Writers Competition, Heinemann Educational Books, 1982; *Young Writers Two – 24th Year*, H.E.B., 1983; *Our Lives*, ILEA English Centre, 1979; *Hey, Mr. Butterfly*, edited by Alasdair Aston, ILEA, 1978

The Aggie Match

Lynne Reid Banks, *One More River*, Puffin, 1980; *The Farthest-Away Mountain*, Abelard Schuman, 1976; *The Indians in the Cupboard*, Granada, 1981; *I, Houdini*, Granada, 1981; *The Writing on the Wall*, Puffin, 1982; *Maura's Angel*, Dent, 1984; 'Trust' in *The Real Thing: Seven Stories of Love*, Bodley Head, 1977

Acknowledgements

The editor and publishers wish to thank the following for permission to reprint the short stories:

Faber and Faber Ltd for 'May Queen' from *Dog Days and Cat Naps* by Gene Kemp

Gervase Phinn for his previously unpublished story 'The Last Laugh'

Merle Hodge for 'Jeffie Lemmington And Me'

Faber and Faber Ltd for 'How the Elephant Became' from *How the Whale Became and Other Stories* by Ted Hughes

Ralph Prince for 'Sharlo's Strange Bargain'

Faber and Faber Ltd for 'Joe's Cat' from *Dog Days and Cat Naps* by Gene Kemp

Penguin Books Ltd for 'Lenny's Red-Letter Day' by Bernard Ashley from Bernard Ashley: *I'm Trying to Tell You* (Kestrel Books 1981) pp. 59–79. Copyright © 1981 by Bernard Ashley

Jonathan Cape Ltd and Penguin Books Ltd for 'The Hitch-hiker' from *The Wonderful Story of Henry Sugar and Six More* by Roald Dahl

Penguin Books Ltd for 'The Choice is Yours' by Jan Mark from Jan Mark: *Nothing to be Afraid of* (Puffin Books 1982) pp. 31–43. Copyright © Jan Mark 1977, 1980

Heinemann Educational Books Ltd for 'The Toad' by Melanie Bush from *Young Writers 24th Year* (W.H. Smith)

The author Lynne Reid Banks and the author's agents Watson, Little Ltd for 'The Aggie Match'

Unwin Hyman English Series
Series editor: Roy Blatchford
Advisers: Jane Leggett and Gervaise Phinn

Unwin Hyman Short Stories
Bright Streets, Dark Corners edited by David Harmer
Crimebusters edited by Barry Pateman and Jennie Sidney
Crying For Happiness edited by Jane Leggett
Dreams and Resolutions edited by Roy Blatchford
First Class edited by Michael Bennett
It's Now or Never edited by Jane Leggett and Roy Blatchford
Openings edited by Roy Blatchford
Pigs is Pigs edited by Trevor Millum
School's OK edited by Josie Karavasil and Roy Blatchford
Shorties edited by Roy Blatchford
Snakes and Ladders edited by H. T. Robertson
Stepping Out edited by Jane Leggett
Sweet and Sour edited by Gervaise Phinn
That'll Be The Day edited by Roy Blatchford

Unwin Hyman Collections
Free As I Know edited by Beverley Naidoo
Funnybones edited by Trevor Millum
In Our Image edited by Andrew Goodwyn
Northern Lights edited by Leslie Wheeler and Douglas Young
Solid Ground edited by Jane Leggett and Sue Libovitch

Unwin Hyman Plays
Right On Cue edited by Gervaise Phinn
Scriptz edited by Ian Lumsden
Stage Write edited by Gervaise Phinn